Fayette

A Time to Leave

Donna Winters

Great Lakes Romances®

Bigwater Publishing
Garden, Michigan
greatlakesromances.com

Fayette—A Time to Leave
Copyright © 2009 by Donna Winters

Great Lakes Romances® is a registered trademark of
Bigwater Publishing, 4555 II Rd., Garden, MI 49835

Library of Congress Control Number: 2009903285

ISBN: 978-0-923048-91-4

Edited by Pamela Quint Chambers
Printed in the United States of America

First Printing June 2009

Chapter

1

Sac Bay, Michigan
Spring, 1885

Cold drizzle fell from heavy clouds, dampening fourteen-year-old Violet Harrigan's red curls and running in rivulets down her icy cheeks, but she hardly noticed. Her focus remained steadfast on the open grave before her. The coffin lying at the bottom contained her father's broken body, the life crushed out of him in a tree-felling accident less than twenty-four hours ago. She seemed incapable of grasping that horrible truth.

To her right, her stocky brother, Dan, age twelve, held the hand of their petite ten-year-old sister, Rose, who had been crying constantly since learning of Papa's death. Their mother huddled close, attempting to calm her youngest while struggling to control her own grief.

Violet had never known her mother to be so distraught. Her bitter sobs upon hearing of her husband's misfortune had been more than Violet could bear. Thankfully, her mother's kin from Fayette, a few miles north, had come the moment word reached them, and had been very comforting.

The townsfolk had helped, too, preparing the grave, coffin, and body for burial and providing meals for the family. Violet shifted her focus to the opposite side of the grave.

How thankful she was for the presence of her lifelong friends and next-door-neighbors, Celina Legard, who was also fourteen, and her twenty-year-old brother Guy. Their blue eyes, normally sparkling with the joy of life, today appeared almost as gray as the sky. Twelve-year-old Joseph Legard, Dan's good pal, was there, too, his narrow face looking glum. Their parents and four more brothers and sisters soon joined the other three Legards creating a sea of black berets attesting to their French Canadian heritage—all except Guy's older brother, Louis. For reasons unknown, he had put off his beret in favor of a small black Stetson a couple of years ago. Until then, he and Guy had looked almost like twins with their matching hats and mustaches, and their strong, wiry build.

With the last of the mourners gathered near, Violet's maternal grandfather, Angus McAdams, stepped to the foot of the grave, pulled his brown tweed cap from his balding head, and addressed the gathered company with a hearty, yet solemn voice. "Let us bow our heads."

But Violet seemed incapable of that simple act, her neck rigid—her whole body, in fact, frozen in a moment of fear for what was to become of her family without her beloved papa. Unbidden, her feet took flight, carrying her away from the graveside service, through trees and down a long, weedy path to the shore of Sac Bay. Just as a wave crashed on the beach sending sand into a swirl of confusion, a surge of anger exploded within.

Face skyward, she shook her fist in the air.

"Why, God? *Why?*"

Her only answer came from gulls crying and circling overhead.

With a prolonged shriek of rage, she sank to her knees and let the tears come. Trembling with uncontrollable sobs, she barely noticed the splashing of foam and sand onto her black woolen skirt. Then a pair of strong hands began lifting her and she knew without looking that they belonged to Guy, the one who had been closer than a brother for as long as she could remember.

"Come, *ma petite amie*, my little friend." Guy's heart was breaking at the profound sorrow of his cherished friend. He guided her to a beached log where they sat, her head against his neck, his arm about her shoulders until she could cry no more.

Drying her tears with his handkerchief, he lifted her chin and studied her pale, troubled countenance. "Listen to me, *ma petite amie*." He spoke tenderly. "Have I not been watching out for you from the beginning?"

She nodded, her liquid brown gaze meeting his and melting his heart with the pain and sorrow he found there.

He continued assertively. "And it will be ever so. I promise."

Fourth Monday of June, several weeks later.

The portly store proprietor set two pounds of sugar beside the five pounds of flour on the counter and addressed Violet's mother. "Anything else this afternoon, Widow Harrigan?"

"That will be all, Mr. Ansell. Would you please put it on my account?"

Ten-year-old Rose tugged on her mother's black crepe sleeve. "Mama, aren't you forgetting something?" An impish gleam lit her brown eyes when she pointed to the jar of peppermint candy sticks.

Lavinia smiled beneath her black veil. "I did promise

you children candy sticks if you were good and finished your lessons and chores on time this past week. You may help yourselves."

Rose wasted not a second moving a candy stick from the jar to her mouth, as did her older brother Dan.

Violet hung back.

Lavinia's brow furrowed. "Are you feeling all right, Violet? I haven't known you to pass up a candy stick."

"I'm all right, I'm just not hungry," Violet said indifferently. She wanted to say that there wasn't enough candy in the entire store to sweeten the sour mood she'd been in since Papa passed away.

While the storekeeper bent over his ledger, Dan wandered off to admire the catcher's mitt displayed on a nearby shelf. But Rose edged nearer the ciphering proprietor, observing as she sucked her peppermint stick.

He set down his pencil and smiled at her beneath his bushy mustache. "Young lady, I suppose you and your brother and sister are looking forward to summer recess the end of this week."

Rose removed the sweet from her mouth with a smack and flipped back her carrot-colored braid with the toss of her head. "We'll be right pleased for school to be over, Mr. Ansell. Did you know my sister's graduating from the eighth grade?" Her freckled face beamed.

"Doesn't seem possible," declared the proprietor, taking a peppermint stick from the jar and extending it to Violet. "Congratulations, young lady! This one's on me, in honor of your graduation."

Violet was about to refuse when she noticed that the clank of the candy jar lid and Mr. Ansell's offer had attracted her brother like a magnet. He was watching her carefully while the shopkeeper continued.

"I know you're not hungry, Miss Violet, but this peppermint stick has got your name on it and I can't very well put it back, can I?"

Violet glared at Dan, and then accepted the candy with a quiet word of thanks.

Lavinia turned to the children. "Will you three please wait for me outside? I'll be there in a minute."

Violet ushered her brother and sister into the bright sunshine, letting the screen door slam behind her. Then she instantly turned back, slipping silently inside. Hidden by the display of yard goods, she sucked on her peppermint stick, hoping to learn something of the graduation gift her mother had in mind for her. What she heard was not at all what she was expecting.

"Thank you for carrying my account since my husband passed away, Mr. Ansell. I want you to know that I intend to pay it off at the end of the week. Mr. Elliott has agreed to buy my horse, cow, and chickens. Then I'll be in to settle up."

"Thank you for letting me know," Mr. Ansell said kindly, "but how will you get on without any milk or eggs for that growing brood of yours?"

"We'll be fine. After Violet's graduation, I'm moving with the children up to Fayette to live with my mother and father."

Violet nearly choked on her peppermint stick at the news of the move.

Her mother continued in a hushed voice. "Please don't mention it to the children, Mr. Ansell. I haven't told them yet."

"Your secret's safe with me," the storekeeper promised. "I want you to know that you and the youngsters will be missed by us Sac Bay folks. After all, you've been here how many years now? Birthed your children right there in that house your husband built."

Lavinia spoke matter-of-factly. "We'll miss being here, but I have no choice."

Mr. Ansell said, "I understand the Fayette Furnace is scheduled to shut down soon, according to Saturday's paper. But you probably already knew that, with your kin employed there."

"I hadn't heard."

Violet detected a note of alarm in her mother's three short words.

The storekeeper continued. "No telling how long the furnace will be out of blast, according to the paper. Fayette could be in for rough times, but for your sake and your family's, I hope it doesn't come to that."

"So do I, Mr. Ansell, so do I. Good day, sir."

Violet swiftly slipped out the door, desperate to keep her emotions—and her words—in check for the time being. The half-mile walk home seemed more like ten miles as she struggled to come to grips with the prospect of leaving the only home she'd ever known, and her best friends, Celina and Guy. The very thought of it turned the peppermint stick sour in her mouth. Eager to be done with it, she chewed and swallowed so quickly she nearly choked.

At home, she waited until Dan and Rose had been sent outside to weed the garden, a job Violet detested, then she went to the kitchen intending to confront her mother about the plan to move. But the sight she beheld gave her pause.

Sunshine from the window backlit auburn hair that lacked its former shine. Silent tears coursed down her mother's sad face as she filled the flour bin. When she swiped at her cheek with the back of her floury hand, fine white dust drifted onto the black widow's weeds that had

8

been her costume since Papa died. How Violet missed the pretty calico dress her mama used to wear, and the sparkle that had gone out of her once lively brown eyes. Dark circles now rimmed them beneath, and when Violet went to hug her mama, the slim firmness of her bony frame made Violet long for the soft fullness of former days.

Violet shed tears of her own as she held her mother close, and when they parted, she dried her mama's careworn countenance with the gentle touch of her lavender-scented handkerchief.

In a futile attempt to smile, her mother offered gratitude choked with grief. "Thank you, dear. I needed that hug more than ... " Again, she sobbed, and again Violet embraced her mother's trembling form, putting aside a discussion about their move until a more appropriate time.

The occasion rose after supper. Her brother and sister had gone fishing with Joseph Legard, Dan's best friend, leaving her alone with her mother who was seated in her rocker with her mending.

Pulling a straight chair near, Violet spoke with concern. "Mama, may I talk to you?"

Evidently sensing the seriousness of Violet's concern, Lavinia lay down her mending and focused on her daughter. "Of course, dear, anytime. What is on your mind?"

Violet drew a deep breath, lowered her gaze, and spoke regretfully. "I owe you an apology for eavesdropping on you and Mr. Ansell this afternoon at the store. I know I shouldn't have, but ..." She raised her chin and looked directly into her mother's eyes. "Why didn't you tell us we're moving to Fayette?"

"I ..." She blinked several times. "I didn't want to worry you, dear, and I didn't want the thought of moving to spoil your last week of grammar school. After all, graduation from the eighth grade comes only once in a young person's life." She reached for Violet's hand, giving it a squeeze. "I'm very proud of you, dear, and the fine example you set for your brother and sister."

With words of thanks, Violet eased from her mother's grasp to wander to the opposite side of the parlor. Whirling around, she pleaded, "Why do we have to move? Why can't we stay here?"

Her mother rose. "Come and I'll show you."

Violet followed her mother to the kitchen where she reached to the highest shelf for the old cookie jar that held the family cash. Removing the lid, she tipped the empty container toward Violet. "We have no money now that your papa's gone. I can't support you and your brother and sister here in Sac Bay. At Fayette with your grandparents, we'll have a roof over our heads and food on the table."

"But Mr. Ansell said the furnace is shutting down. 'Fayette could be in for rough times,' he said. Can't we stay here? I could hire myself out to cook and clean and take care of children. Then we wouldn't have to move!"

Lavinia shook her head with remorse. "There's no work to be had here, dear. I've already inquired. But I'm glad you're willing to help out. Perhaps we'll both find work at Fayette once the shutdown is over. And God willing, it will be sooner rather than later."

"But I don't *want* to go to Fayette. I want to stay *here*. I've lived all my life here. All my friends are in Sac Bay. It's the same for Dan and Rose. We can't leave here. We just can't!"

Determination shone in her mother's brown eyes. "I'm sorry, Violet. We're moving on Saturday and that is that." Her words were clipped, terse, final.

Violet whirled around and headed out the door as fast as

her feet could carry her. Unmindful of her direction, she ended up at the beach, sitting on the very same log where she had sat on the day her father had been buried. Just as she had not been able to grasp the loss of her father, neither could she grasp the fact that Guy and Celina and the rest of the big Legard family would no longer be her neighbors. Her world was falling apart and she was powerless to stop it! She buried her face in the handkerchief still damp with her mother's tears and let the sobs come, wondering if she would ever live past this season of sadness. She had no idea how long she had been crying when she felt the gentle touch of a hand on her shoulder and heard the sweet voice of Celina.

"*Ma chère,* my dear, hush now."

Violet looked up to find that Guy was there, too. She struggled to get words out. "We…we…we're moving to Fayette!"

Celina nodded sadly, her watery blue eyes almost gray with regret. "Your mama came and told us."

"We'll never see each other anymore!" Violet lamented, new sobs erupting.

Her friends sat on either side of her, and then Guy's strong hand enfolded hers. "*Au contraire,* on the contrary. I will bring my sister often to visit you. And Joseph, too, to see Dan. And I will be making charcoal deliveries to the furnace for Papa from time to time." Guy referred to the contract his father, a collier or charcoal maker, had long held with the Jackson Iron Company to supply fuel for the iron smelting operation.

Violet spoke through her tears. "But the furnace is shutting down. The newspaper said so."

Celina made a quick reply. "No matter. We promised your mama we would weed her garden and bring her the ripe vegetables as often as we could."

Violet pulled her hand from Guy's and dried her tears. "But why do we have to move? *Why*? I'd do all the weeding myself if only we could stay here!"

Her friends laughed, knowing how she hated that job. Violet even chuckled at herself.

Celina tossed back her brown hair. "If only your mama could hear you now!"

Guy raised a finger of caution. "But I do not think she would change her mind about moving, even with such an offer."

Violet drew a breath to argue but Guy continued.

"It is a hard fact, *ma petite amie*, but you will be better off at Fayette." The words cut a hole in his very own heart, but he would not shrink from the truth. Wrapping a comforting arm about her, he continued. "Your family is not like ours. When the furnace shuts down for a time and Papa cannot sell charcoal, my older brothers and I do a little farming and fishing and hunting to see us through. But the same is not so for your mama. She is wise to take you to your grandmama and grandpapa. Your grandpapa has worked for the Jackson Iron Company for so long, they would have to go out of business before he would be out of work!"

"Guy's right," Celina said. "And think of this—your Uncle Toby and Aunt Elin, and your Uncle Sven and Aunt Flora are at Fayette, too." She named Violet's mother's kin, each couple with children of their own.

"But I don't want to move away!" Violet insisted.

Guy squeezed her shoulder and released her, gazing directly into her brown eyes. "Remember when I taught you to clean a whitefish, how you hated it?"

Violet nodded.

"But now, you clean a whitefish in no time and barely give it a thought. It will be so with moving to Fayette. You hate the thought of it now, but you will soon get used to living there."

"Fayette stinks worse than a whitefish!" Violet claimed, remembering her many visits to her grandparents' and the acrid smell of furnace smoke that permeated the entire village and beyond.

"The smell will be gone with the furnaces dead," he reminded her.

Celina nodded. "Guy is right, *ma chère,* and he is wise to say you will get used to life there. Besides, I will pray to God. He will help you!"

Only the earnestness in Celina's face and voice prevented further argument, but Violet was too disappointed with God to expect any good thing to come from Him, or from leaving Sac Bay.

Chapter

2

Fayette—nearly eleven weeks later
Saturday evening, September 5

Tablecloths in hand, Violet paused on the back stoop of her grandparents' home to observe the happy commotion taking place on the lawns of her grandparents and their neighbors, Lars and Greta Lindberg. Soon, the two families plus Guy, Celina, and Joseph Legard, who had come to stay the night, would gather for supper around the long outdoor table overlooking the harbor. Then all would be peaceful and orderly, but for now, a myriad of voices and activities filled the yard.

Around the maple tree, her ten-year-old sister, Rose, chased two-year-old cousins, Kal and Mary Grace, who screeched with delight when she caught them and tickled them silly. Violet held no doubt that Rose had become their favorite cousin after this summer of daily fun and games.

A safe distance south of the toddlers, the clang of a horseshoe circling a stake rang out, followed by the victorious shouts of twelve-year-old Dan and his friend Joseph Legard. Violet smiled at their victory over Uncle Toby and Uncle Sven, an achievement the boys had been striving for since the end of June. With a prayer in her heart, Violet silently thanked God that the two Fayette uncles had restored energy and cheerfulness to the withdrawn, glum-faced brother who had moved here two months ago.

A few feet from the back stoop, Aunt Flora, who was big with child, engaged in a sedate game of beanbag toss with the four-year-olds, Ola and Ingrid. When Aunt Flora caught the bag atop her belly, the little ones squealed with joy and begged her to do it again.

Beneath their glad voices rumbled Lars Lindberg's deep-chested laugh at some innocent joke Grandpa McAdams had shared with him and Guy over the fire pit where they broiled whitefish caught earlier in the afternoon. It was good to hear the old Swede laugh—a sound that had been all too rare since the furnace shutdown at midnight on the third of July. Unlike her grandfather and Uncle Sven, who worked daily on the repair of the furnaces, Lars and Uncle Toby had not earned a day's pay in eight weeks. Worse yet, the Lindberg boarding house had emptied of all but Lars and Greta. In addition, the Jackson Iron Company had offered no news on when they would again fire up the furnaces and hire laborers to fill the Lindberg beds.

Perhaps the lack of work for both Lars and Greta had prompted their idea yesterday for tonight's big family gathering. The normally industrious couple seemed a tad bit at loose ends this summer and none the happier for it, from Violet's observation.

Despite the lack of regular employment for most, summer at Fayette had proved far more agreeable than Violet had imagined upon her arrival at the end of June. She and Dan and Rose had been quickly absorbed into the midst of family life as if they'd always been here. No two days were the same with two sets of aunts and uncles and four cousins under the age of five living on the next street. Someone always needed a hand with children or help in the kitchen or a fishing partner to go catch dinner.

Tonight's meal would be a rare feast in these lean times, Violet knew. Since the halt of furnace work, the unemployed that had remained at Fayette hunted and fished out of necessity to put food on the table. Supper tonight would be bountiful and tasty, nonetheless, with harbor fish plentiful and garden crops ripe for the picking. Guy, Celina, and Joseph had succeeded beautifully with the Sac Bay garden, bringing melons, cucumbers, and tomatoes as they ripened throughout the summer. This morning they had brought a large basketful of the fresh produce that would find its way to the supper table.

The garden next door had produced well also, with Lars available to weed, water, and harvest. At this very minute Greta and Elin were busy in the Lindberg kitchen making the best of his produce. Violet inhaled the tantalizing smell of fried onions and garlic that would spark up the boiled string beans. A hint of Greta's raspberry turnovers was also detectable on the soft harbor breeze. The very thought of that delectable confection made Violet's mouth water.

From the McAdams kitchen behind her wafted two equally delicious aromas—that of the chicken and bean cassoulet that her dear friend Celina Legard had helped Grandma to prepare, and the essence of her mother's taffy tarts fresh from the oven. Violet could almost taste the rich brown sugar filling and light flaky crust that, according to family legend, had convinced her grandfather to marry her grandmother, and her father to marry her mother. She was still contemplating that thought when her mother emerged from the door behind her, a basket of napkins and silverware in hand.

"Violet, haven't you spread the tablecloths yet?"

"I'll do it right now, Mama."

Together they stepped off the stoop and headed for the

long table fashioned of boards on barrels.

Ingrid dropped the beanbag and followed after them. "Cousin Violet, where are you going?"

"We're going to set the table, Ingrid. Would you like to help?"

She nodded, her blond braids bouncing as she ran barefoot ahead of them. Violet's unexpected joy this summer had been four-year-old Ingrid, the elder daughter of Uncle Toby and Aunt Elin. Her inquisitive mind and affable personality had led to a special bond, and seldom a day went by without some contact between them.

Now, she helped Violet spread the picnic cloths across the boards until they hung evenly on both sides, and together they began setting out knives, forks, and spoons. Elin joined them with settings for the Lindbergs. Within a few minutes, plates, tumblers, and pitchers of fresh well water had been added to the settings.

With the cooking, baking, and broiling completed, platters, casserole dishes, and trays heaped with goodness took their places down the center of the table. Then Lars called everyone to the feast in a voice so loud, it echoed off the bluff.

"Careful!" Grandpa Angus warned with a grin. "You'll have everyone in town joining us!"

The tall Swede chuckled and rested his big mitt of a hand on Angus's shoulder. "I think ve are the only ones left in the village. The others are down the road, drinking their supper." He referred to the tavern outside of town.

Soon all had gathered at the table. The two-year-olds sat on the laps of their mothers. The four-year-olds perched on cushioned chairs across from Violet. Her cherished friends Celina and Guy flanked her on either side.

Lars and Grandpa Angus took their seats at the head and

foot of the long table, and then Lars asked a blessing in deep, solemn tones.

"God, thank you for this food and this family. In Jesus' name, Amen." He raised his head and gazed at the gathering before him, deep grooves carving a countenance so sad, Violet thought for a moment that tears would spill from his pale blue eyes. Then he reached for a platter of fish, put on an unconvincing smile, and declared, "Let us begin!"

Violet took a small portion of every dish that passed her way—broiled whitefish, cassoulet, string beans and onions simmered with herbs from Elin's garden, and fresh tomatoes and cantaloupe from Sac Bay. While the ladies complimented one another on the cooking and baking and exchanged tips for tasty recipes, conversation among the fellows included cryptic talk of the best fishing holes and hunting spots. By the time the cookies and taffy tarts had made their way around the table, Grandpa and Lars had challenged each other to a game of horseshoes.

Grandpa said, "Whoever wins can take on a new challenger until we have a champion. I even have an old broom I'll present to the winner. You can tie it to your chimney!" He referred to an old custom amongst various blast furnaces in Upper Michigan to award a broom to the one producing the most iron for the week.

Lars chuckled. "That vould be the only vay a broom is von in Fayette these days."

Uncle Toby pushed back his blue tweed cap. "I may have lost at horseshoes before supper, but now that I'm stoked up with reinforcements, I'm ready to take on the winner of the first round."

Dan said, "Then it's my turn."

Joseph said, "And then mine!"

Guy said, "And then mine!"

Sven said, "I'll show you all who is best!"

Angus said, "That, you will—when you lose to *me!*"

Four-year-old Ola said, "What about me?"

Lars said, "You may ride on my shoulders vhen I vin the broom! Come, now. Ve start." Rising from the table, he paused. "I nearly forget. After horseshoes, Greta and I bid you all come to our place for coffee and cookies, ja?"

With a general acceptance of the invitation, the fellows left the table to begin their horseshoe challenge.

Grandma smiled and pushed back a silver strand that streaked her dark hair. "That leaves us ladies to clear and clean up. I suppose we'd best get started."

While Greta and Elin tended to their chores next door, Violet, Celina, and Ingrid helped Grandma in the McAdams kitchen. Meanwhile, Flora and Rose watched over Kal and Mary Grace, eventually lulling them to sleep on the floor of the parlor. Violet was putting away the last of the clean dishes when she heard a commotion outside.

Rushing to the window, she discovered Lars. With a broom in one hand, he balanced little Ola on his shoulders with the other and sang a little song. "I von the broom! I von the broom! Now don't you like my little tune?" Behind him followed the others.

Violet picked up Ingrid so she could see, and then called Grandma and Celina to the window to watch the victory parade that paused outside.

With a broad smile, Lars announced, "I von the broom!"

Grandma said, "So I see! Congratulations!"

"Now come to our house. Coffee and cookies are vaiting. And I have something important to tell you. Come *now, ja?*"

Grandma began untying her apron. "We'll be right there. Should I bring the leftover taffy tarts?"

Lars nodded vigorously. "*Ja,* good. Bring those vonderful tarts!" Turning toward home, he began singing his victory song again.

Violet set Ingrid down, and commented. "Your grandpa sure is happy!"

Smiling from braid to braid, the little girl nodded.

Grandma chuckled softly. "I don't think I've ever seen Lars so talkative. What could he have to tell us, I wonder?"

Celina said, "It must be something good. He's too jolly for bad news."

Grandma nodded. "You are right, my dear." To Ingrid, she said, "Would you please run to the parlor and tell Flora and Rose we're going to the Lindbergs now?"

She hurried off. Before Grandma had finished filling a plate with tarts, Ingrid returned, speaking in hushed tones. "Aunt Flora and Cousin Rose are asleep. So are Kal and Mary Grace."

Grandma spoke quietly. "Then we'll let them sleep." Draping a fresh sack towel over the tarts, she said, "Let's be on our way!"

At the Lindbergs', the long boarding house table soon filled with family and friends, Celina and Guy taking seats either side of Violet. Greta and Elin quickly poured coffee for the adults and lemonade for the children, and passed the heaping plates of brown sugar cookies and tarts.

The fellows were all abuzz about their horseshoe contest, telling how ringers had been knocked aside and leaners had been toppled by Lars to gain him the final victory over his longtime rival, Angus McAdams.

Laughing at his loss, Grandpa said, "Lars, this was a great idea you and Greta had—a big family dinner and then a horseshoe contest that keeps everyone guessing until the last toss. We ought to do this all over again next Saturday.

What do you say?"

The smile quickly faded from the old Swede's face, replaced by the melancholy Violet recalled seeing at the dinner table. His blue eyes swam in unshed tears while he cleared his throat. When he spoke, the low tone carried a funereal heaviness.

"I said I had something to tell you. It is this." His gaze slowly swept down one side of the table and up the other, settling on Angus, to his right. "Ve are leaving Fayette. Greta, and me, and your son Toby and our daughter Elin, and Ingrid and Mary Grace—all of us are going to Wisconsin, to our kin, to start a dairy farm."

Grandpa McAdams gasped. "No, Lars!" He turned to his son. "Toby, tell me it isn't true!"

Uncle Toby hung his head in silence.

Violet's heart went out to him. How well she knew the pain of an unwanted move.

Lars pulled his handkerchief from his pocket to cover his face for a cough that Violet knew was an excuse to dry his tears. Clearing his throat, he spoke again, his voice quiet yet unwavering.

"Angus, my friend, ve cannot stay here any longer. Ve have no vork. Ve have no hope of getting any vork."

Grandpa McAdams ran his hand over his balding head. "I'm sure the furnaces will fire up again, or the Jackson Iron Company wouldn't be paying me and Sven and some others to make repairs."

Toby spoke. "Papa, it's good that you and Sven have work, but Lars and I are finding it harder and harder to make do without pay week after week. It's been two months now, and my savings are gone except for enough to buy passage to Wisconsin."

Grandma said, "I don't see how you'll start a dairy farm

with no cash."

Lars said, "Greta and I—ve have enough money saved to buy dairy stock. Our kin have plenty of pastureland. They vant us to come."

Greta nodded. "They have wanted us to come for years. Now, it is time."

Lars added, "Ve leave one veek from tonight on the *C.W. Moore*."

The finality of his statement sent a numbing chill through Violet, despite the warmth of the evening. Across the table from her, little Ingrid sat on her mother's lap asking if they really were going to Wisconsin. Elin quietly assured her that she would love living there with her aunts, uncles, cousins, and lots of cows.

Lars' words, *Ve leave one veek from tonight…* rang in Violet's ears, their significance weighing heavy on her mind. The family unity that had served to heal her wounded heart here at Fayette was about to be torn apart and the pain of new losses was already setting in. Celina and Guy, ever sensitive to her emotions, each grasped one of her hands in theirs. Violet silently thanked God for their comforting touch and abiding friendship, then berated Him for permitting new suffering to cross her path again.

Chapter

3

One week later at Fayette
Late afternoon on Saturday, September 12

Dan tapped Violet soundly on the shoulder and took flight, calling back over his shoulder. "You're it, Sis!"

Violet whirled around and tagged her best friend. "*You're* it, Celina!" Taking off like a shot, Violet ran head-long into Guy.

"Careful, *ma petite amie!*" His strong arms steadied her and released her to continue her escape in the rollicking game of tag that included several of the town's kids. She circled behind the Machine Shop, pausing to catch her breath and peek out at the bustle of activity at the center of town. There, boards on sawhorses made long tables where her mother, grandmother, aunts, and a dozen other ladies of the community were busy spreading cloths and setting plates, cups, and silverware for a community supper.

The celebration would mark the departure of Violet's Uncle Toby, Aunt Elin, and their daughters, along with Elin's mother and father, Greta and Lars Lindberg. In a way, her Grandpa McAdams had gotten his wish for another big dinner, but it would not end with a hotly contested game of horseshoes. Instead, about three hours from now the steamer *C.W. Moore* would carry precious family and friends to Wisconsin.

But Violet couldn't think of that now. Dan was headed her way again, intent on tagging her for the second time. Unable to escape, she ran after her sister, Rose, an easy tag, then circled behind the Town Hall where she paused to think. Gazing out across the harbor, she tried to imagine life at Fayette without her kin and neighbors.

She thanked God that school had started for her younger brother and sister. Otherwise, Dan would hardly know what to do with his time. He had spent nearly every day with Uncle Toby fishing, hunting small game, rowing around the harbor, practicing his pitching, catching, and hitting, and exploring the bluff. Since the furnace shutdown, her broad-shouldered uncle in his nifty blue cap, and her shorter, stockier brother with his flyaway red hair had made a commonly seen pair in the village.

As for her sister, Rose, Violet knew she would miss Mary Grace terribly. What a wonderful cousin she had been to the wee, blonde two-year-old, watching over her, playing with her, singing her to sleep at nap time most afternoons.

But it was the lithe, delicate Ingrid that Violet worried about the most. At four years of age, she was old enough to feel the loss of the only home she had known. Violet prayed that the shy little girl would make the adjustment to Wisconsin and that God would ease the painful loss for both of them.

She prayed for her Aunt Elin and Uncle Toby, too, that they would be successful in dairy farming. How dearly she would miss her fair, willowy Aunt Elin and her angelic ways. She had taught Violet how to make her special Swedish bread called Limpa bread, and how to cook white-fish with a tasty cream sauce. In the last few days, Violet had sadly helped to pack the family's chests and sell unneeded possessions.

The sound of the dinner bell pushed that unhappy thought from her mind and she hurried to find her place at the table between Celina and Guy. Bowing her head, she joined hands with them while Grandpa McAdams, seated at the head table several feet away, said grace.

"Almighty God, we ask Thy blessings upon the food we are about to receive, and the loved ones who are about to depart from our midst. Deliver these travelers safely to their destination and shower upon them Thy gifts of peace and prosperity in their new endeavor. In the name of Your precious son, Jesus, we pray. Amen."

"Amen," echoed around the table, followed quickly by the hum of conversation and clank of serving pieces against bowls and platters. Ham, smoked whitefish, fried chicken, and potato salad passed Violet's way, followed by fresh sliced tomatoes, cucumbers, cantaloupe, and pickles from her mother's garden in Sac Bay. The Legards had brought yet another load of fresh produce this week, and tonight they would stay over at the empty boarding house, arising tomorrow to attend services at the Fayette church before returning to Sac Bay.

Violet loved these weekend visits, as did her brother, Dan, who sat opposite her beside his best friend, Joseph Legard, whose dark wavy hair seemed to be forever falling down across his forehead. The two of them pursued their supper with hearty appetites, and time passed quickly as Celina and Guy delivered news of Sac Bay, laughing at tricks Louis, their older brother, had played on neighbors.

When Violet bit into a slice of fresh, juicy cantaloupe, she was grateful once again for the gardening efforts of the Legards, watering, weeding, harvesting, and delivering. The succulent sweetness of the melon satisfied her appetite for dessert, causing her to pass up the sugar cookies, taffy tarts, and apple pie that came her way.

With dessert nearly over, her Grandpa McAdams, seated at the head table with the departing families and the furnace superintendent and his wife, rose and clapped two pan lids together to get everyone's attention.

"I would like to say a few words in honor of our friends, neighbors, and family members who will be departing this evening for greener pastures across the bay. Lars—" Angus turned to gaze regretfully at the strapping Swede seated beside him. "—I'm sure I speak for all that know you. We're real sorry that after all these years, you'll be leaving the State of Michigan and our 'pigs' to take up life in the State of Wisconsin with her cows." The clever reference to pig iron brought chuckles.

Angus continued. "We'll sure miss you and Greta—and of course your daughter, my son, and our grandchildren who are going with you." He referred to his own son, Toby, and family. "I couldn't have asked for better neighbors or in-laws. God be with you, my friend." Angus's voice broke at the very end.

Lars rose to his feet, wrapped his arm about Angus's shoulders in a brief, manly hug, then faced the audience. "I am not much for speeches, but this I must say. I vill miss you all." He made a wide sweep with his arm. "But like the Apostle Paul once said, 'I have learned in vhatsoever state I am, therevith to be content.' So, vhether in the State of Michigan or the State of Visconsin, I vill be all right."

Words of farewell and blessings came from the audience as Lars returned to his seat.

Violet, having listened intently to the big Swede's profession of faith, wondered if she would one day be able to say the same thing of herself.

That thought was interrupted by the voice of her grandfather, who was on his feet again, a cigar box in hand.

"Lars, my good man, we're not done with you yet. On behalf of the entire community, I'd like to present you and your family with this farewell gift." Lifting the lid for all to see, he revealed a box filled near to overflowing—not with cigars—but with coins and paper money. Angus pushed the big Swede's dinner plate aside and set the open box in front him.

Lars shook his head in disbelief, slowly closed the lid, then opened it again and shook his head some more. Rising to his feet, he motioned for silence. "Thank you!" He spoke with an emotion-choked voice. Hand over his heart, he repeated, "Thank you! From the heart!"

Reactions varied from applause and whistles to shouts of, "We'll miss you, Lars," and "Come back and see us sometime."

When all was quiet, Angus introduced the Company Superintendent, Harry Merry. As he rose to speak, Violet felt anger rising within toward the short, broad-chested official who had ordered the furnace shutdown. It was all she could do to keep from shouting her frustration at him for the difficulties he had caused—people moving away, families separated, lives upset. Biting her tongue, she tried to listen to the man's expression of thanks for loyalty, dependability, and hard work. But anger put her feet in motion, and before she knew it, she was running up Stewart Avenue as fast as she could go, turning off the road when she reached her grandparents' home. Wandering into the backyard, she paced behind the woodshed, spitting harsh words that she was certain only she and a scrawny black cat could hear.

"I hate Superintendent Merry! *I hate him!* If only—"

Her words were interrupted by Guy's calming voice. "Hush, *ma petite amie.*"

She spun to face him. "I won't hush! He could give the order for the furnaces to start up again, then everybody could get back to work. But he won't. Now Uncle Toby and Aunt Elin have to move. It isn't fair! It just *isn't fair!*"

Guy shook his head and spoke quietly, hoping to calm his young friend. "Such is life, *ma petite amie,* such is life."

"You're no help, Guy! Do you know that? No help at all!"

"What would you have me do?" he asked tenderly, an idea coming to him. Quickly, he began tickling her waist the way he had when she was small.

Violet giggled uncontrollably. "Stop! …Please! … I can't … catch my breath!"

"Do you promise not to be angry anymore tonight?"

"I promise! … *Please* … let me go!"

Releasing her waist, he caught her firmly by the shoulders and gazed into her upturned face. Happy tears stained rosy cheeks that framed a wide smile. He patted her cheeks with his handkerchief. "Violet, you are so much prettier when you smile—prettier, even, than your name. Now, come. The others will wonder where we are."

No sooner had the words left his mouth than his sister's voice floated to them on a harbor breeze. "Violet! Guy!"

He replied instantly. "Here, Celina! By the woodshed."

She rounded the corner of the house, hurrying toward Violet. "*Ma chère,* are you all right?"

Violet nodded, ready to explain, but Guy spoke first.

"She had lost her jolly and came up here looking for it."

Celina grinned, her blue eyes sparkling. "And did you find it?"

Violet shook her head and laughed. "Of course not. But no matter. Guy tickled me a new one."

"Thank goodness for that! Now, we'd better go back,

before your mother worries." Celina started for the road against loud protestations of the stray black cat that blocked her way and meowed hungrily. "Shoo! Go away! I will have bad luck if you cross my path!"

Violet quickly scooped the slender feline into her arms. "You don't really believe that old superstition do you? She's just hungry. I'll get her a bowl of milk."

"Is she yours?" Celina wondered.

Violet shook her head. "Not exactly, but she's been trying awfully hard to adopt us for the past week. Here, you hold her while I go inside and get the milk."

When Celina protested, Violet shoved the creature into Guy's arms and hurried inside. Within moments, the cat was lapping hungrily, allowing Violet and her friends to return unimpeded to the center of the village where townsfolk were bidding a fond farewell to those who were to depart on the *C.W. Moore*. A robust blond man Violet had often seen outside the hotel came along to offer parting words. Big Toby, as the man was called, hugged her uncle as if they were brothers, reminiscing about a time when he had stayed with the McAdams's before he had moved to the hotel to live and work.

Too soon, under dusky skies, the lights of the steamer entered the quiet harbor, then hugged the dock where the Lindberg and McAdams families waited, trunks and bags in readiness for stowage. Violet's family along with her Aunt Flora's family and her grandparents all pressed close to bid their final good-byes.

Violet spoke past a lump in her throat when she hugged her Uncle Toby and her Aunt Elin, who was holding Mary Grace on her hip. But when she came to Ingrid, Violet could not keep the tears from spilling down her cheeks. Seeing the unhappy look on that precious girl's face, Violet knelt down, forced herself to smile, and took Ingrid's hands in each of hers. "You and your sister come visit us soon, all right?"

Ingrid nodded solemnly.

"Now smile for me," Violet encouraged, giving a gentle tug to the tike's blonde braid. "You don't want me to remember you with that sad look on your face, do you?"

Shyly, the little girl beamed a smile, then hugged Violet's neck.

Violet wrapped her arms about Ingrid, kissed her cheek, then released her and turned to go, hurrying off the dock and across Harbor Street in an effort to outpace the melancholy that was nipping at her heels. When she reached the grassy rise above the water, she watched while the steamer cast off and chugged out of the harbor, and she wondered how many more times Fayette families would leave to find their fortunes in fairer fields.

Chapter

4

One month later
Monday, October 12, 1885

The morning scripture reading in the parlor now over, Violet's grandmother folded her hands on her open Bible, bowed her graying head, and began to pray while Blackie, the stray cat that had come to stay, lay purring by her feet.

"Heavenly Father, we thank Thee for Thy Holy Word and the promises You have given us. You know the desires of our hearts, that Your protection would remain over us and all our family, near and far. Guide us in paths of righteousness that we may keep sin far from us. And *please* bring us word from our kin in Wisconsin, Father. All this we ask in the name of Thy beloved Son, Jesus. Amen."

"Amen," echoed Violet and her mother.

Lavinia rose. "I'm going to fill the boiler and start the wash. Violet, would you please collect the linens from the upstairs bedrooms?"

"Yes, Mama."

Before they could get as far as the parlor door, the rattle of a cart outside and the barking of a dog sent Blackie streaking past them and up the stairs to hide.

Grandma hurried to the window, pushing aside the lace curtain. "Look! Flora has brought her little ones in the dog-cart. Big Boy is pulling it, and Pet, Rocky, and Jack are following behind." She named Flora's four cherished canines, and then paused to look more closely. "Flora is carrying a little dog in her arms. I hope she hasn't taken it into her family, what with her baby about to make an appearance any time now." Grandma headed for the front door, grabbing her black cape from the hall tree on the way.

Violet and her mother reached for their capes and followed Grandma into the bright sunshine and gentle breeze of this slightly crisp fall day.

Grandma wasted no time speaking her mind to her very pregnant daughter. "Flora, I *do* wish you'd stay at home. I'm sure you'll deliver soon. I was just about to come and see if you needed my help today." Pointing to the small dog, she continued without a pause. "And whose is this, pray tell? Not yours, I hope."

"Good glory, no!" Flora shook her head, strands of sandy hair coming loose from her bun to frame her oval face. Stroking the pup, she explained. "This fellow is a recalcitrant little stray on his way to a new home. Would you please watch Ola and Kal while I take him down to the dock?"

Grandma fixed her with a stern look. "I don't think you should go down there, Flora. Your delivery date has already passed and you're carrying that baby awfully low now. Your pains could start at any minute."

Flora smiled. "I know, but I've got to go and see the tug captain. This rogue has been scaring horses all over town, and digging holes big enough to break their legs. I've got to convince the good captain to take him on board as his mascot. If I don't get Rascal out of town today, Superintendent Merry is going to have him shot. Now how could I let that happen to a fellow with a face as charming as this?"

For as long as Violet could remember, her Aunt Flora had been finding homes for the stray cats and dogs of Fayette. She even kept kennels for them behind her house. Violet couldn't help smiling at this stray, with his bearded gray terrier-like face topped by perky ears that flopped over at the very tips.

Lavinia spoke up. "Violet and I will go with Flora, Mama. It won't take but a few minutes. We'll check at the Post Office for a letter from Toby before we come home."

Grandma's scowl softened at mention of a stop at the Post Office. "As you wish." She lifted Ola, then Kal from the cart. "You know I love having the boys here." To the little ones, she said, "Should we go inside for some cookies and milk?"

Gleefully the boys headed indoors with their grandmother.

Flora set the small dog on the ground, commanded him to sit, then handed his leash to Violet. "He's an escape artist so hold tight while I unhitch Big Boy from the cart. It wouldn't do to let Rascal loose in the village again."

Rascal tugged and chewed on his leash, refusing to stop until Violet picked him up.

With Big Boy unhitched, Flora commanded her four dogs to heel and headed down to the dock. Violet and Lavinia followed, impressed by the discipline of Flora's pets when they ignored a stray cat that crossed their path. Rascal, on the other hand, nearly jumped to his freedom in an effort to chase. Violet barely managed to keep her hold on him, suffering a few minor scratches in the struggle.

At the dock, Flora commanded her four dogs to lie down and stay, took Rascal into her arms, and approached the company tug, greeting the captain who was adjusting one of his lines.

"Good morning, Captain! A mighty fine day we're having on land and lake, wouldn't you say?"

"Good morning, Mrs. Jorgensen! It is a fine day indeed! I see you've got your faithful friends with you, and some kin as well." He smiled in the direction of Violet and her mother. "Good morning ladies!"

"Good morning, Captain!" they replied in unison.

He turned to Flora. "And who is this little fellow in your arms? A new member of your canine crew?"

"No, sir. I'm hoping you'll make him a member of *your* crew—your mascot, companion, and vermin exterminator for your days on the water and your nights in port."

The captain stroked his graying beard.

Flora went on. "He's a great mouser, a ferocious protector, and a fine alarm bell. Best of all, he'll be your faithful friend and affectionate, loyal, and true until death do you part."

"Is that so?" The arch of skepticism curved one bushy brow.

"That *is* so," Flora replied confidently. "Of course, he'll have to get to know you, and in order for that to happen, you'll have to keep him tied to the tug at first, just until he learns not to roam."

"I see," said the captain, reaching toward Rascal.

Rascal whined with excitement and licked his hand as if they were old friends.

Flora held the dog out to him. "He's just begging you for a new home. How can you refuse a face like his?"

Reluctantly, the captain took Rascal in his arms. The dog immediately licked his cheek. "I don't suppose I could say no to such a fine fellow as this."

"Then it's settled!" Flora concluded cheerfully. With a note of caution, she added, "Now, don't you dare let him loose while in Fayette. Superintendent Merry gave me this one day to find Rascal a home out of town, otherwise he was going to have him shot for harassing horses and digging holes in the streets."

The captain groaned. "*Now* you tell me!"

"You'll have smooth sailing if you keep him tied onboard," Flora reminded him. "Good day, Captain!"

"Good day—I think—Mrs. Jorgensen."

Flora turned in the direction of the Company Store and Post Office, Violet and Lavinia beside her. At Flora's command, the four dogs followed. Commenting casually, she said, "It would certainly make Mama's day if we could hand her a letter from—" Suddenly she grimaced and bent forward. Hands supporting her belly, she muttered through clenched teeth. "Good glory, Livvy! I think…"

Lavinia's arm went instantly around her. "Is it the baby?"

Flora nodded. Her four dogs, sensing a problem, formed a tight circle about them, nudging in on all sides.

When Flora's pain subsided, she straightened and stroked each dog. "I'm fine, my faithful friends. Now we'd better go home."

Lavinia spoke with urgency. "I'll go with you. We'll send Violet for Dr. Phillips and Sven. Do you want Mama to come? Violet can take care of Ola and Kal until Dan and Rose get home from school to help her."

Flora nodded and turned to Violet. "Your mother's right. Please go now and do as she says!"

On winged feet Violet headed into the village, passing the General Store and Post Office to go straight to Dr. Phillips' office. He was not there, but a sign said he could be found at home. On she went to the Machine Shop where Sven immediately dropped what he was doing.

Next, Violet hurried up Stewart Street to Dr. Phillips' place, delivering the request that set the medical man to packing his bag. Then, she went home to tell her grandmother the news.

Grandma shook her head. "I just knew it! Are you sure you'll be all right with Ola and Kal?"

The two boys were playing with the wooden train cars that had been their Uncle Toby's. "We'll be fine. Now go, and don't give us another thought."

Grabbing her cape from the hall tree, she disappeared out the door.

Violet joined the boys on the floor, helping them to hook together the six cars of the train and move it across the rug. The biggest challenge was convincing Kal to leave the cars connected rather than picking them up and tossing them across the room. After several futile attempts, Violet gave the red caboose to Kal, set him aside, and then helped Ola with the other five. Several minutes passed while Ola's train made stops at imaginary charcoal kilns to pick up fuel for the furnaces and bring it to Fayette. Kal seemed content to run his caboose across the floor on a different path. Both boys were *choo, choo*ing with great gusto when Grandma returned unexpectedly.

Violet rose quickly to greet her in the entry hall. "Did Aunt Flora have her baby already?"

Grandma shook her head. "No, but all is well—*too* well. With your mother, Dr. Phillips, and Sven on hand, I was just in the way. So I thought I'd spend the day getting some things accomplished here at home." She removed her shawl and hung it on the hall tree.

"Are we going to do the laundry?" Violet asked.

Grandma turned to her with a grin. "Oh, no, my dear. I have something *much* more enjoyable in mind."

"What's that, Grandma?"

"Baking taffy tarts! Did you know it's a family tradition?" Her arm about Violet, she ushered her into the parlor and they sat on the sofa. "When your mother was born, your great-grandmother baked taffy tarts to celebrate. She did the same when your Uncle Toby and Aunt Flora were born. Then, when you and your brother and sister and each of your cousins were born, I baked taffy tarts."

"I remember now," Violet said thoughtfully. "When Rose was born, you came to stay with us to take care of Dan and me, and I helped you. When we were all finished, you let me roll out the leftover dough for cinnamon-sugar pinwheels."

"That's right! Hard to believe that was ten years ago when you were only four."

Just then, Ola said gleefully, "Gramma! Look!" With great care he began pulling the train—all the cars including the caboose—around the room, *choo, choo*ing as he crept across the floor on his knees.

Kal, unhappy over the loss of his toy, headed for the bright red caboose, hand extended.

"No, Kal!" warned Ola, giving his younger brother a shove before he could grasp the coveted toy.

Kal landed on his bottom with a thud and loud cries that brought Violet to his rescue.

Scooping him into her arms, she returned to the sofa to cuddle him, and in no time he grew quiet.

Grandma smiled. "Looks to me like you've got everything under control here with the boys. I'm going to start on lunch. Your grandfather will be home before we know it! We'll do our baking while the boys take their afternoon naps."

While the boys slept in a fort made of sheets draped over chairs in the room off the kitchen, Violet measured and sifted the flour and salt, then worked in the lard and ice water for the crust and began rolling it out. Meanwhile, her grandmother mixed the brown sugar, butter, vanilla, and egg for the filling, and told stories of the births of her own children.

"The first is always the hardest," she recalled. "I thought Lavinia would never arrive. Finally, after a day and a half, she made her grand appearance with a head full of red hair. Flora, on the other hand, came very fast—in about three hours—and was nearly bald."

"What about Uncle Toby?"

"Ah, yes. Toby." Grandma grew thoughtful. "That boy has always had a mind of his own—right from the day of his birth. He had us all worried when he presented himself feet first. But he came out all right and I was none the worse for it." She paused, her countenance melancholy, her voice hushed. "I only wish I knew if he was all right way over there in Wisconsin."

Violet drew a sharp breath. "Grandma, I forgot to check for a letter. With all the excitement about Aunt Flora, we never made it to the Post Office."

Grandma's face brightened. "Go right now. I'll finish the tart shells and get them into the oven while you're gone."

Violet set aside the rolling pin, untied her apron, and hurried to the front entry. Grabbing her cape, she swung open the door and almost ran headlong into Sven.

The slim Norwegian stepped inside, his clean-shaven face beaming. "We have a daughter! She is *beautiful!* Where is Mary? Flora asked for her."

"She's in the kitchen."

He pulled his brown plush hat from his head and started down the hall.

Violet hung up her cape and followed him.

When he had announced the good news to Mary, Violet said, "Grandma, you go with Sven. *I'll* finish the tarts and stay with the children."

Grandma appeared skeptical. "Are you sure?"

"Yes! Go!"

Violet was removing the last of the tarts and the cinnamon-sugar pinwheels from the oven when Ola and Kal awoke from their naps. After a snack of pinwheels and milk, she took them on a walk to the Post Office. Her hand trembled when she discovered a letter from Wisconsin. Tucking it into her cape pocket, she returned home and played with Ola and Kal until Dan and Rose arrived from school.

Enlisting Dan to entertain the boys and Rose to help in the kitchen, Violet began preparing an evening meal of scalloped potatoes and ham. The dining table was set and dinner was in the warming oven when Grandpa returned from the furnace and Grandma came home from Flora and Sven's. The older woman's face glowed as everyone gathered around to hear of the new baby.

"She is absolutely *perfect!* So like her mother, except not quite so bald. Her head is covered with blond hair that is softer than peach fuzz."

Grandpa smiled. "And how is Flora doing?"

"Just fine!" Grandma replied. "We can all thank the Lord that both mother and child are healthy and happy."

Rose said, "Has Aunt Flora chosen a name yet?"

Grandma nodded. "Hope Fayette."

"Hope Fayette," Grandpa echoed. Picking up four-year-old Ola, he said, "You have a new little sister named Hope Fayette. What do you think of that?"

Ignoring the question, Ola asked one of his own. "Is it time for supper? I'm hungry!"

Dan said, "So am I!"

Kal said, "Cookie?"

Violet shook her head. "Not now, Kal. Supper is ready."

When everyone had gathered at the table, clasped hands, and bowed their heads, Grandpa prayed. "Almighty God, we thank you for Hope Fayette, for Flora's good health, and for this food we are about to eat. Bless this food to our use, and watch over all our family. In Jesus' name, Amen."

"Amen," echoed the others.

Grandma looked thoughtful. "I'll write to Toby and Elin in care of her kin and tell them about Hope Fayette. How I wish that boy would write us a letter. I'm not even sure he received the others I sent."

Violet excused herself and hurried to the hall to fetch the letter in her cape pocket, returning quickly to hand it to her grandmother.

When she saw the postmark, she drew a sharp breath. Tearing open the flap with shaky hands, she read silently, then aloud.

"'All is well. We are all healthy and happy and so are our twenty cows!'" Grandma read on about the trip to Wisconsin, the work on the dairy farm, and the start of construction on a home where Toby and his family would live with Greta and Lars. Returning the missive to its envelope, she said, "This has truly been a wonderful day! A letter from Toby and a new baby to give us hope."

Ola spoke up. "Hope Fayette, Grandma!"

She smiled. "Yes, Ola. Hope Fayette!"

Silently, Violet thanked God for the blessings of the day, praying that the new baby's name, Hope Fayette, would have true meaning for the future of this idle furnace town.

Chapter

5

Fayette, seven months later
Mid-April, 1886

"Celina! Look!" Violet cried. The moment her friend turned toward her, Violet let the pillow fly.

Celina ducked, covering her dark head with her arms.

The pillow sailed past her into the hallway, hitting Violet's mother soundly in the midsection.

With lightning reflexes, Lavinia caught the pillow, stepped into the doorway of the boarding house bedroom and fixed a stern look on Violet.

"I'm sorry, Mama! I didn't mean—"

Before she could even finish apologizing, her mother's offended look changed to a mischievous grin and she sent the pillow back to Violet with a well-aimed toss of her own.

Violet caught it easily but before she could return the shot, her mother had picked up a second pillow from the stack on the bed and rushed toward her, a determined look in her brown eyes.

"You naughty girl!" She laughed, and began spanking Violet's derrièr with the feather pillow.

Giggling, Violet spanked back.

Celina came after her friend to give a pillow spanking of her own.

"Shame on you, Celina Legard!" Violet laughed, swinging the pillow at her.

Lavinia followed suit. "Yes! Shame on you, Celina! This is all your fault!"

"*Moi? Au contraire, Madame!*" Celina protested. Unable to withstand the assault, she collapsed on the bed in laughter.

Violet turned again to her mother, trading pillow whacks with her until they, too, fell on the bed in a heap of giggles.

When the laughter had died down, Lavinia sat up, wiping happy tears from her cheeks. "I haven't laughed this hard since … "

Violet knew what her mother was thinking. She hadn't laughed this hard since Papa died. But Violet wasn't about to give voice to those words. Instead, she said thoughtfully, "It was good to hear you laugh again, Mama."

Lavinia smiled and gazed down at her fondly. "And it was good to hear *you* laugh."

Celina propped herself up on an elbow, her blue eyes twinkling. "And to think it was all my fault!"

Violet giggled. "Yes, *your* fault, Celina!" She pushed her friend's elbow out from under her and the two of them laughed some more.

Still smiling, Lavinia rose to her feet and wagged a finger at the two. "I guess I'll know who to blame if our work isn't done on time." Turning serious, she reminded them, "This boarding house is supposed to be ready for guests in two days. We still have to clean the place thoroughly, air all the towels, sheets, blankets, and pillows, and make up all the beds, not to mention moving our belongings from Mama and Papa's and unpacking them." She referred to her folks' home next door where she and her children had been living for several months.

43

Violet hopped to her feet, observing with a smile, "At least these three pillows have been aired!"

Celina rose and scooped up an armful of bed linens. "Come, Violet. Help me air these sheets outdoors. I will not be the cause of delay for your mother's new boarding house business!"

Without hesitation Violet sprang from the bed, grabbed some blankets, and followed her friend downstairs and outside. The smell of furnace smoke and the clang of hammers on pig iron again filled the air after months of idleness. The birth of Hope Fayette and the meaning of her name had indeed signified a change for the better. With the furnaces hungry for fuel, Celina's father and brothers could again sell their charcoal, bringing enough money for her oldest brother, Augustus, to get married and buy the Sac Bay house that Violet's family had left vacant nearly a year ago.

Here in Fayette, furnace men were returning to work and needed a bed to sleep on and meals to eat. Her mother had arranged with the Jackson Iron Company to reopen the boarding house that had been closed by the Lindbergs before their move to Wisconsin. But her mother couldn't do it alone. She was relying on Violet's help to make the business successful. As Violet shook a blanket in the fresh air blowing in from the harbor, she was determined not to let her mother down.

For the rest of the morning and into the afternoon, she and Celina helped to air the linens, dust the furniture left behind by the Lindbergs, mop the floors, and wash down the kitchen walls. Meanwhile, next door, Rose and Grandma McAdams had been packing trunks and crates. By late afternoon, all was in readiness for the move.

Guy, Dan, and Joseph, who had spent the day catching fish for the evening meal, returned to carry belongings to the boarding house. Soon, Dan's trunk had been hauled to the attic where he would have his own, private quarters. The ladies' trunks and bags lined the master bedroom on the first floor, off the kitchen. The parlor, with its bare floor and sparse furnishings, echoed with Violet's footsteps when she passed through to open the front door. There, Dan and Joseph were waiting with a chest of household goods—the maple chest with the heart that her father had carved into the lid. The sight of it sent a pain of longing into Violet's own heart.

Guy entered behind Dan and Joseph with a heavy crate. Setting it beside the chest, he stooped to pick up the whistle that lay on top, and turned to Violet with a sentimental smile. "I remember well how your papa could chase cares away with the tunes from this whistle. When he played, everybody danced!"

Dan came alongside and drew the whistle from Guy's hands. His brown eyes thoughtful, he studied it for a moment, then put it to his lips and began to play *The Galway Piper*, stopping the instant he saw his mother enter the room.

Though her eyes glistened, she smiled and insisted with words and gesture, "Play on, Son!" At the sound of the first note, she lifted her skirt and began the heel-toe dance of the jig, her face lighting with pleasure.

Guy cast off his black beret and took Violet by the hand. Then, as they had done since childhood, they too danced the jig.

Celina, who had gone outdoors to bring the laundry in from the line, quickly set clean clothes on a bench and took up the jig with her nimble younger brother, Joseph.

Violet couldn't remember the last time her feet—and her heart—felt so light. The room awhirl with dancers, she could see her father smiling down from heaven and hear him clapping time to the rhythm. For the next few minutes, as long as the whistle was playing, Papa's spirit was right there, flooding her with happy memories that banished all sadness.

Too soon, the jig was up. Her mother, a little out of breath, brushed a loose strand of brown hair from her rosy cheek as she approached Dan. "I'd forgotten how good it is for the soul to dance. Thank you for reminding me, Son!" Patting her brow with her handkerchief, she gazed at the crate and trunk. "I suppose we must get on with the unpacking now, but promise me, Son, that you'll play for us again real soon, won't you?"

"Of course, Mama!" With a satisfied smile, he polished the whistle on his shirtsleeve and carefully set it back in the crate.

As Violet bent to pick up the laundry that needed folding, she heard the front door open, followed by the panicked voice of Rose.

"Mama! Come quick! Something's wrong with Grandma!"

Chapter

6

Heart pounding, Violet dropped the laundry to rush after her sister. Through Grandma's front door and down the hall to the kitchen they flew.

The sight that greeted Violet there made her gasp. On the floor in a heap by the stove lay her grandmother, struggling weakly to gain her feet while Blackie stood guard, meowing in distress. Violet knelt beside her grandmother and pushed the cat aside. "Grandma! What happened?"

Her grandmother struggled silently to reply while Lavinia and the others gathered around her.

Rose tried to explain. "Grandma was stirring the fish stew when all of a sudden, for no reason at all, she fell straight to the floor. I tried to get her up, but I just couldn't!"

Lavinia knelt beside Violet. "Mama, can you speak? Can you tell us what's wrong?"

Her lips moved slightly, but only an unintelligible moan came out. Pushing with her left hand, she tried to sit up, but quickly fell back.

Lavinia turned to the boys. "Guy, Dan, please help her to her bed."

One on each side, they carefully raised her up, carried her to the master bedroom next to the kitchen, and laid her on the bed.

Lavinia thanked them and issued new requests. "Dan, please run to the casting house and tell your grandfather what's happened. Guy, would you be so kind as to fetch Dr. Phillips? And Joseph, I'd be much obliged if you'd draw a bucket of fresh water from the well and set it just outside the bedroom door while the girls and I tend to Mama."

"Yes, Ma'am."

Celina volunteered to tend to the stew and biscuits that were being prepared for dinner while Violet and Rose assisted their mother in the bedroom. While removing Grandma's dress and helping her into her nightgown, it became obvious that, besides being unable to speak, Grandma had lost the use of her right side. Seeing this normally active, articulate grandmother suddenly helpless and completely dependent troubled Violet so much, it was all she could do to keep from running out of the room to cry. But she would not abandon her beloved grandmother in her time of need. Instead, she focused on the task at hand, pouring fresh water from the bucket outside the door into her grandmother's wash basin and sponging her face with a cool washcloth.

Her grandmother tried to smile, but only the left corner of her mouth turned upward, bringing a lump to Violet's throat and tears to her eyes. She turned away, determined not to let her grandmother catch her crying. Regaining control of her emotions, she plumped her grandmother's pillow, kissed her cheek, and excused herself to make a trip to the outhouse. Thankfully, by the time she finished there, her grandfather and Dr. Phillips were in the bedroom with Grandma while everyone else, including her mother, waited in the kitchen for the examination to be completed.

A collection of glum faces filled the room. The boys and Guy sat at a small table, each munching on a biscuit meant for dinner, now delayed. Rose and Celina worked at the baker's cabinet, cutting out another batch of biscuits to go into the oven. Lavinia stood at the stove mindlessly stirring the stew that smelled strongly of fresh fish and onions while Blackie pressed against her ankles and meowed. On any other occasion, Violet would have been ravenously hungry, but the thought of eating was far from her mind when she approached her mother and spoke quietly into her ear.

"Mama, what do you suppose is wrong with Grandma? Why can't she talk?"

With a deliberate shake of her head, Lavinia continued stirring while she answered. "I don't know, dear. Maybe Dr. Phillips will have an answer." Suddenly, setting the spoon aside, she turned to the others. "We need to pray. Please, can we all join hands?" When the circle was complete and heads were bowed, her mother began.

"Heavenly Father, we don't know what's wrong with Mama, but you know, and you can heal her. We ask now that you place your hand upon her body, mend whatever needs fixing, and make her whole. Thank you, Father."

Guy continued the prayer with similar sentiments, some in English, some in French. His brother and sister followed suit. Dan prayed, then it was Rose's turn.

"God, you know everything, and you can do anything. Hear our prayers and help Grandma to walk and talk again."

Last of all, Violet prayed, pouring out her heart to her Maker. While she was speaking, Guy prayed silently for his young friend, asking that she would not have to suffer yet another loss on the heels of those that had gone before.

Violet had not yet finished her prayer when the bedroom door opened. She brought her earnest petition to a close. "...so *please*, God, I *beg* you, restore Grandma to full health. In the name of your precious son, Jesus, Amen."

Grandma's voice, steady and strong, announced, "Your prayers are answered!"

"Grandma!" Violet rushed to her, as did the others. Everyone was full of questions.

"Are you all right?"

"What happened?"

"Are you *sure* you're all right?"

"Maybe you should sit down."

Guy brought a chair.

Grandma waved it off with a smile. And this time, *both* sides of her mouth curled upward. "It was just a spell. I'm fine now. Really! Except for one thing."

A flurry of inquiries followed, to which she responded, "I've got an appetite that won't be satisfied with anything less than a good helping of that fish stew on biscuits. So while I'm getting out of this nightgown and robe and back into my day dress, I hope you all will be setting the table. It's way past time we sat down for dinner, you know." She turned to her husband and the young doctor who were standing behind her. "Doc, I sure appreciate your coming. I'm fine now—back to my old self again. You're welcome to stay for dinner."

When he declined the invitation, she said, "Angus, will you please see him out? I'm going to get ready for dinner." And with that, she disappeared into the bedroom.

Lavinia turned to the others. "You heard Grandma! Boys, will you please make sure we have enough chairs at the dining table to seat everyone? Girls, please bake the last tray of biscuits, set the table, and pour the stew into the tureen. I'm going to talk with Dr. Phillips."

Violet turned to Celina and Rose. "You heard Mama. Get busy. I'll be back in a minute to pour the stew into the tureen." Heading to the room behind the kitchen known as the Maple Room, she joined her mother and grandfather just inside the back door where the slim, dark-haired doctor had set down his bag and was offering his learned opinion.

"Like Mary said, it was just a spell and nothing more. But that doesn't mean it couldn't happen again, or turn into something more serious."

Grandpa said, "Like a stroke?"

The doctor's brown-eyed gaze held more than a hint of sorrow. "I remember when you called me to tend Mary's mother a few years back."

Lavinia sighed. "One day, she was perfectly healthy. The next, she couldn't walk, talk, or eat. A week later, we buried her."

Dr. Phillips nodded. "Keep your eye on your mother for the next few days and send for me if she has another spell. I don't mean to scare you, but often these tendencies run in families." He bent to pick up his bag.

While Lavinia and Grandpa saw Dr. Phillips out, Violet turned toward the kitchen, her thoughts a-whirl. The loss of her great-grandmother had been quite a shock. Violet couldn't bear to think that the same thing could happen to Grandma.

At the sound of the bedroom door opening, Violet hurried to give her grandmother a tight hug. "You gave us an awful scare! I'm so glad you're better, Grandma!"

"Me, too, dear. Me, too." Releasing from the embrace, she smiled broadly and gazed steadily into Violet's eyes. "Now forget about that. It's time we all sat down to enjoy some fish stew!"

Violet forced the corners of her mouth upward. "You're right, Grandma. I'll pour it into the tureen and bring it to the table."

A couple of minutes later, everyone gathered around the dining table for the evening meal and Grandpa McAdams said grace. He thanked God for the food they were about to eat, for Grandma's good health, and for the prosperity her mother would experience in her new boarding house business. Though eager to embrace his optimism, Violet couldn't ignore the sense of uneasiness that washed over her. Would she drown in the insecurities of her changing world, or rise above them once again to inhale the breezes of hope, confidence, and success?

Chapter

7

Fayette, eighteen months later
Saturday, October 29, 1887

Leaving the hard work of her mother's successful boarding house behind, Violet settled on the Legards' wagon seat between Guy and Celina while her brother climbed into the back with Joseph. As Guy drove out of Fayette, conversation turned to the evening of fun at the husking bee her friends had been telling her about for the past month. When they arrived at the Richbourg farm where the event was to take place, the happy chatter of young people was spilling from the large open door of the barn. Pulling the wagon into the empty cornfield beside several similar rigs, Guy hopped down and assisted Violet. His strong hands about her waist, her hands atop his solid shoulders, he set her gently on the ground. A chilly breeze whipped across the open land, teasing at the hem of her red gingham dress, but when she would have turned to follow Celina, Joseph, and Dan inside, his grip lingered. She gazed up and discovered a look that surprised her. Beneath the black beret, his blue-eyed gaze held an intensity that hinted at more than the brotherly affection to which she was accustomed.

Guy paused to study the young woman that Violet had become at age sixteen. Seemingly overnight she had matured from the gangly, petulant girl of earlier years to the shapely, graceful creature now looking up at him with questioning brown eyes. His heart skipped a beat. In that instant he released her waist, caught her by the hand, and together they hurried toward the sounds of merriment.

This was Violet's first husking bee. Although Guy, now twenty-two, had been attending such events for several years and had told her what to expect, the sights inside the cavernous barn far exceeded her expectations.

Yellow corn shocks were piled high against the walls— so high that Violet couldn't imagine an army, let alone a gathering of young people, husking them all. Festoons of aromatic cedar hung above them, as did lanterns that cast their soft yellow glow on bright, happy faces. From heavy rafters drooped fringes and tassels of pine, their clean scent mingling with that of the hay stacked in the mow. Violet drew a deep breath of the sweet aroma, then searched the heights for the cedar wreath of which Guy had spoken. Finding it high up in a corner of the peaked roof, she silently vowed not to be caught beneath it unawares, lest a kiss be stolen from her before she was willing to bestow it.

"Guy! Over here!" Joseph's voice from across a circle of corn shock seats interrupted the thought. Guy and Violet took their places beside him and Dan. Joseph's blue eyes sparkled beneath the tight band of his black beret, his gaze firmly on his older brother. "Bet I can shuck more corn tonight than you can!"

"*Au contraire, mon frère.* This is your first husking bee. I have been attending for some six years now. We shall see who can shuck more corn!"

With that, the brothers commenced their work, fingers flying as they discarded husks and tossed golden ears over their shoulders into a pile at their backs. Violet grabbed an ear of corn and began to work in earnest, but even at her very fastest, she could shuck only one ear to every one-and-a-half or two that Guy tossed into the pile.

While she worked, she took in the company around her. Across the way, Celina sat not far from eighteen-year-old Chase Simmons, a mild-mannered, slender framed Sac Bay native who had caught her fancy of late. From the looks of Chase, who often stole glances at Celina and sent smiles her way, the feeling was mutual. Though Chase was not one to enter into the bragging and boasting of the young swains around him, Violet could understand her friend's attraction to his quiet, unassuming demeanor.

A few feet from Chase stood Buck Turkle, his opposite in nearly every way. Big and broad, bold and blustery, he seized every opportunity to boast. One foot propped on a hay bale, he shucked corn while bragging of his latest accomplishments. Violet need listen for only a short while to learn that he had harvested more corn, baled more hay, picked more apples, and shot more deer than any living soul on the Garden Peninsula. When anyone tried to counter his claims, Buck quickly responded with a cutting remark. So predictable were his replies, it soon became obvious that others were simply baiting him.

Violet smiled at the banter, as did Sam and Sadie Schutt and the two Henry sisters who sat to her left. The Schutts and Henrys were former schoolmates from Sac Bay, and while the Schutts had remained just as slim as Violet remembered them, the Henry sisters had changed considerably in the past two years. Hannah's and Harriet's formerly slim figures had filled out to a fair degree of plumpness, but their sweet smiles remained pleasant as ever, framed between round, pink cheeks.

Reaching for another shock of corn, Violet wondered

who would be the first to discover a red ear. Guy had warned her that any girl finding one must hold it high and run. The fellows would follow in hopes of being the first to catch her and claim the kiss that was due, lips on lips. Violet had never been kissed on the lips by Guy or anyone else. She was pondering the predicament of having to kiss someone as distasteful as Buck Turkle when a cry went up and Celina began weaving in and out among the workers, red ear held high like a torch.

Half a dozen young admirers began to follow. Around and around they went. One by one, Buck shoved his competitors, including Chase, aside and continued pursuit.

Celina was slowing down, dodging between piles of shucked corn and stacks of shocks, pausing to catch her breath, then darting forth when Buck discovered her hiding place.

Finally out of wind, she scrambled atop some hay bales piled half a dozen high against the wall and gazed down at him. "I … give … up."

"And now for my kiss!" he announced triumphantly. Placing his foot on the first bale, he glanced back at the onlookers, a smug grin on his face.

Violet's heart went out to her friend, whose look of dread spoke a thousand words.

Buck paid no heed. Intent on collecting his prize, he continued his ascent, unaware that behind him, Chase was climbing the ladder to the haymow and reaching for a rope that had been tied to a rafter.

When Buck was two steps below Celina, Chase came swooping down. Aiming for the bale in between the two, he made a slight miscalculation, bumping his rival in a way that sent Buck tumbling to the floor and landed Chase on his backside immediately below Celina.

Whoops and hollers filled the air.

Chase scrambled to his feet and stepped up beside Celina. Gazing at her with true tenderness, his lips gently descended to hers.

Cheers went up from all but Buck, who rose to his feet, dusted himself off, and glared up at Chase. "You thief! You stole the kiss that was supposed to be mine! I'll get you for it, you little scoundrel! Now come down here and face me like a man!" Buck shook his fist in the air.

With a nervous smile, Chase said, "I do apologize for putting you off balance. That was not my intent. As for the kiss, I won it fair and square."

"You *cheated!*" Buck accused.

Chase shook his head. "All's fair. There's no rule against rope swinging, is there?"

Guy spoke up. "No rule at all." Rising to his feet, he approached Buck, resting a hand on his shoulder. "Come, *mon ami.* Much work must yet be done before we get a taste of Mrs. Richbourg's famous pumpkin pie."

The appeal to Buck's stomach succeeded, and he returned to husking with nothing but a low grumble and a brief backward glance.

Time passed with congenial conversation and flying fingers that continued to deplete the pile of shocks. The incident with Buck was all but forgotten when Violet pulled back the shuck of a corncob to discover the undeniably red color of its kernels. Raising it high, she bounded off.

Weaving between the workers, she cast a backward glance. Buck was in the lead. When Guy tried to pass, Buck pushed him away, landing him on a pile of shucked corn.

Angry and determined, Guy scrambled to his feet. He would not let Buck or anyone else claim Violet's first kiss.

With a burst of speed he headed straight for her, hopping over corn shucks and leaping across bails of hay in an effort to cut Buck off. He had gained the lead when his foot slipped on a stray corncob sending him down once more.

Again he rose to continue the chase. Violet was clearly running out of speed, and when she glanced back to find Buck closing in, her look of revulsion tore at Guy's heart, infusing him with renewed vigor.

But before either Buck or Guy could catch up to her, she managed one last burst of speed and darted to the corner by the corn heap. Out of breath and as frightened as a rabbit before hounds, she tossed the red ear aside and reached for one of the festoons, climbing and pulling herself to the top of the tall pile.

Determined as a bull, Buck started up after her. He was halfway there when the corn shocks began to give way. The harder he tried to climb, the more he slipped. Grasping at a festoon, he snapped it like a thread. The entire pile stirred beneath his feet. In a great avalanche, Buck went sliding downward. Then Violet slid, too.

Chapter

8

Just when it seemed certain that Violet would land beside Buck at the bottom of the heap, Guy snatched her from the fall. Pulling her into his arms, he lowered his lips to hers.

Violet closed her eyes, catching the essence of clove as Guys mouth covered hers, sending a ripple of buoyant warmth to the very tips of her fingers and toes. When they parted to the whoops and hollers of all but Buck, the sensation lingered, making her feel lighter than air. Resuming her place beside Guy, she took up yet another shock of corn, and while she shucked cob after cob, her thoughts remained on her first ever kiss and the tingle that thrilled her yet. And when she glanced his way, she no longer saw the brotherly fellow she had always known. She saw instead the handsome young man who had claimed her kiss and her heart as well.

Such thoughts lingered until another whoop went up and Hannah Henry took off holding a red ear high. Her short, stocky legs carried her with surprising speed around the circle of workers and behind the pile of yellow ears while Buck and four others took up the chase. Weaving in and out, she changed direction several times until only Buck was following. When he was about to catch up, she managed one last burst of speed, climbing atop the bales of hay. Buck charged up after her.

Violet expected Hannah's smile to change to a look of dread, but if anything it turned even sweeter when she gazed up at Buck. Just when it seemed evident that he would claim his kiss, he paused, an unlikely tenderness transforming his expression. A moment later, when his lips slowly descended to hers, it was as if Violet were experiencing Guy's kiss all over again. She welcomed the memory of his mouth against hers, the sweetness of its firm, moist touch. How grateful she was for the long sleeves that hid the goose bumps rising on her arms. She prayed that Guy would not notice the flush that had surely colored her warm cheeks. When she dared to glimpse him from the corner of her eye, she saw that he, too, was caught up in the romantic scene unfolding on the hay bales.

Buck's kiss lingered long enough to elicit a chorus of whistles and calls from his competitors. And when he released Hannah, his countenance revealed that he was completely smitten. Hand in hand, he escorted her down from her perch and led her to a seat beside his to continue shucking corn. Lively conversation resumed but Violet noticed that Buck's voice was no longer heard. Gone were his boastings and bragging. He seldom opened his mouth, and when he did, he spoke only to Hannah in tones too low for anyone else to hear. She must have found his words to her liking, for whenever he leaned close to whisper into her ear, she giggled softly and blushed and gazed up at him with sparkling eyes.

Their little *tête-à-tête* continued until the work was done and the time for refreshments had arrived. While Violet went with the other girls to fetch the food, Guy assigned the young, first-time huskers to the tasks that awaited their hands. With great enthusiasm they assisted the older fellows in clearing away shucks, carrying out baskets of golden corn, and bringing in boards and barrels to make one long table.

Hannah and Harriet spread bright checkered cloths and set cups and forks in place. Then came a parade of young ladies from the farmhouse bearing tins of pumpkin pie topped with generous dollops of whipped cream, plates of brown doughnuts warm from the fryer, jugs of cider newly pressed, and aprons full of red and golden apples freshly-picked. In no time, makeshift seats of corn shocks surrounded the table and the young gentlemen took their places while the ladies served.

The enticing aroma of fresh doughnuts must have held special appeal for Buck. Guy watched from the other end of the table while the larger fellow piled five of the round treats onto a plate already laden with a generous helping of pie. But no one dared protest and there were doughnuts left over when they had made their first round.

With Violet at his side, Guy tucked into the pumpkin pie, savoring the rich creaminess, the flavorful blend of spices, and the flaky crust that had made it a favorite at gatherings of the locals. The barn grew curiously quiet while consumption took precedence over conversation. When first helpings had been consumed, polite requests for second helpings surfaced and the buzz of conversation gradually resumed.

But Violet was unusually quiet. Though she sat close beside him, the dreamy expression on her face implied that her thoughts were miles away. In addition, the pie on her plate was only half-eaten when others had finished second or third pieces. He leaned close and spoke in her ear.

"Are you feeling all right, *ma petite amie?*"

A smile, nod, and a look of affection that he had never before seen in her brown eyes gave her answer. She slid her pie his way asking him to finish it while she sipped her apple cider. Now, he suspected that her thoughts were not so far away after all.

While savoring her piece of pie, he mentally relished the memory of their first kiss. For years he had dreamt of the time when she would be ready for more than simple friendship. Just as one piece of pie sparked a desire for more, one kiss from Violet had ignited in him a longing for another. He prayed he would be able to curb his appetite until she was a little older. He was pondering that day when some scuffling at the opposite end of the table interrupted his thoughts.

He turned to find Joseph and Dan in a tabletop-wrestling match that had gotten out of hand. Before he could correct them, Buck had them in his sights, voice booming.

"Hey, you two! Behave yourselves! Don't make me come over there and knock your heads together!"

Joseph and Dan sat straight and folded their hands on the tabletop.

Guy had to turn away to keep them from seeing the smile on his face. The tense moment passed quickly. Pleasant conversation resumed while the huskers satisfied their appetites with the last of the pie and doughnuts, and finished off nearly all the cider.

Hastily, the young ladies cleared away cups, forks, empty tins, plates, and jugs and headed back to the farm-house while the gents disassembled the long table, erected a small podium, and cleared the barn floor for dancing. Chase Simmons hauled out his fiddle and mounted the platform with Mr. Richbourg, who was ready to call the dance.

Guy grabbed Violet by the hand and took her to the head of one of the lines for the Virginia Reel. Others in their line included Dan and Celina, Joseph and Harriet, Sam and Sadie, and Buck and Hannah. When all the lines of five or six couples had formed with ladies on one side and gents on the other, Mr. Richbourg started.

"Honor your partner!"

Chase struck up a rousing version of *Durang's Hornpipe* and the bows and curtseys began. Violet felt right at home, having danced the reel many times as a child in Sac Bay, and a time or two at Fayette.

"Forward and turn with the right hand round!"

At the end of the line, Violet noticed that Buck, though slow to start, made up for his speed with enthusiasm.

"Forward again with the left hand round!"

This time, Buck moved exactly in rhythm, returning to his place on beat.

"Do-si-so!"

This back-to-back turn caused some confusion at Buck's end of the line, but he made it to his place in time for the next call.

"Down the center and back!"

This move by the head couple fell to Guy and Violet. He grasped her firmly by the hands and together they side-stepped down the center and back to their places at a lively pace.

"Reel the set! Right to your partner, left to the next!"

Violet swung first with Guy, then with the next fellow in line, who happened to be her brother Dan. Then she swung with Guy again, and on to Joseph. The pattern continued, swinging with Guy and then the next fellow while Guy swung with her, and then the next lady. All went well until Violet came to Buck. He didn't seem to know when his "turn" had ended and kept Violet going in circles until Guy cut in to take Violet on a sidestep move back to the head of the line. They made it there just in time for the march, gents and ladies peeling off to follow their leaders to the foot of the line.

As soon as Violet reached the end of the line, she joined hands with Guy and held them high forming an arch for the other couples to pass through. Pair by pair they ducked under. With Buck and Hannah, it was a tight squeeze and for a moment Violet feared that the arch would split, but Guy held fast and all the dancers moved down the line until Dan and Celina became the head couple. Then the pattern started all over again, repeating until Buck and Hannah had taken their turn as the head couple.

With that round of the reel completed, new groups formed for more dancing. Guy spelled Chase on the fiddle so he could dance with Celina, and Violet paired with Joseph. Over the course of the evening, Dan, Buck, Chase, and Sam all took turns partnering with her, but on the drive home, thoughts of Guy alone danced in her mind.

She snuggled beneath a thick woolen blanket that helped to ward off the damp chill of night. Thankful for the tight press of Guy on one side and Celina on the other, she closed her eyes. In her half-dream state, she relived the evening all over again from the moment Guy lifted her off the wagon outside the barn, to the moment his lips descended to cover hers. A shiver coursed through her that could not be blamed on the cold night air, but Guy must have noticed and thought otherwise, for he momentarily shifted the reins to one hand in order to tuck the blanket more tightly about her with the other.

Violet closed her eyes and returned to her mental meandering, pleased that Guy, Celina, and Joseph would be staying overnight with her grandparents in order to attend church at Fayette tomorrow before returning to Sac Bay.

She looked forward to the big Sunday breakfast she would share with them next door, thankful that her younger sister, Rose, was now old enough to assist their mother with the cooking and serving chores at the boarding house.

In minutes they were back at Fayette. Guy pulled into the yard between the boarding house and her grandparents' and lifted her down from the wagon, then did the same for Celina while Dan and Joseph hopped off the back.

Guy's arm firmly about her waist, he said, "I'll see you to your door."

Dan ran in front of them and into the boardinghouse while Celina and Joseph disappeared into the McAdams home, leaving Guy and Violet alone by the front door. She turned toward him, tilted her face upward, and closed her eyes, imagining his lips descending to cover hers.

Guy's heart thumped. Every emotion within urged him to pull Violet close and cover her mouth with his in a kiss that would last long into the night. But his mind cautioned otherwise. *She is only sixteen. Tonight's spark will start a wildfire that I will regret.* He kissed her forehead and spoke tenderly. "Sweet dreams, *ma petite amie.* I will see you in the morning."

Violet opened her eyes to glimpse Guy swiftly crossing the yard and disappearing inside her grandparents' house. Confused and disappointed, she went indoors, wondering what she had done to break the romantic spell and send him so quickly away.

At breakfast the following morning he was his old brotherly self with no hint of a deeper attraction. Then, after church, before he climbed into the wagon to drive his brother and sister home to Sac Bay, he drew Violet aside. Turning her toward him, he gazed deep into her eyes with a penetrating look that she could not quite define. Was it longing, or regret, or both?

His quiet words gave answer. "Today, I go to lumber camp. I will see you again when winter is over. I will miss you terribly. Can you be a good little girl while I am gone?" He squeezed her hand as if encouraging her to give the answer he sought.

She squeezed back, and although her heart was breaking and tears welled up, she managed a smile. "I can be good, but I'm not a little girl anymore. Haven't you noticed?"

Gently, he ran his finger over her moist cheek. "Indeed I have noticed. You are nearly grown up. And that is making me want to stay near you all the more. But I must go and work and put money by for the future. *Oui*?"

When she gave no answer, he kissed her forehead and quickly climbed aboard the wagon, waving without a backward glance.

Chapter

9

Nine months later
Saturday afternoon, June 16, 1888

As the tug *Jo Harris* left Van's Harbor several miles north of Fayette, Guy leaned over the rail and gazed out across the bay. The sun shimmered on the waves and warmed his weary shoulders. A gusty breeze chased away the smoke from the stack. Drawing a deep breath, he closed his eyes.

A vision of Violet appeared. Red curls framed a sad countenance. Tears slipped from her warm, brown eyes. His heart ached. Their parting moment of last fall had dogged him through his winter in the woods and these last two months at the sawmill in Van's Harbor. No letters had been exchanged but Celina had said Violet was well, and that she had become quite an enthusiastic debater for the Fayette Literary Society. He smiled at the thought, and prayed that she would be as enthusiastic about seeing him again as she had been about her debates.

Then he opened his eyes. Lumber stood in several stacks on the scow alongside the tug. *His* lumber. Hard earned. Enough for a two-room house. He slipped his hand into his pocket and around a thick roll of bills—half the price for forty acres of cutover land in exchange for his winter in the woods. As soon as his lumber was unloaded at

Fayette, he would head to the Jackson Iron Company Office and put the cash down on the parcel next to his brother, Louis's. Like Louis, he would clear the land of stumps for farming.

He bowed his head, closed his eyes, and whispered a prayer. "God, guide me today. You know my plans. You know my heart. Be with Violet, too. And if it's not too much to ask, would you make her happy to see me, *s'il vous plaît? Merci.* Amen."

Fayette, same time

"Celina, won't you *please* come sailing with Reggie and me?" Violet referred to the new friend standing beside her who had arrived at Fayette a week earlier as guest of his aunt and uncle. "You heard Mama. I can't go unless you go, too. Besides, the fresh air and sunshine will do you good, not to mention the excellent company and superb sailing skills that will enhance your experience."

"You sound like this is a debate that you have to win for your side in the Literary Society," Celina commented. Then she glanced down at her copper-colored dress with gold braid trim, and cloth boots to match. "But I'm all dressed up for the dance tonight." She referred to the event to be held in the Town Hall. "I've got to look my best when Chase calls for me at your grandma's. Out in a boat, we're bound to get wet, especially today with the wind and waves. Agnes loaned me this dress," she named an older sister, "and she will be furious if anything happens to it. And Papa just bought me these brand new boots. I'll simply *die* if they get ruined!"

Reggie Vanderveen, a college man from out East, pushed back his straw boater revealing a thick wave of fair hair and sparkling blue eyes. He addressed her concerns with a smile. "Miss Legard, I've been sailing on Long Island Sound since I was too little to remember," he said in an over-confident tone. "I was the commodore of the Yale Corinthian Yacht Club last year. I *promise* you won't get wet. The waves out there are barely breaking whitecaps. The wind is perfect for a great sail! We'll head out to Snake Island." He referred to the small island a short distance from the entrance to Snail-Shell Harbor. "What could possibly go wrong?"

Celina gazed at the island, grooves of skepticism marring her brow beneath the band of her beret.

He continued. "We'll all be back, safe and dry, in plenty of time for supper and the dance. You don't think I'd be fool enough to risk my chances at a marvelous evening with Violet, do you? I'm counting on the taffy tart she promised me for dessert, and a jolly good time at the Town Hall!" He cast a smile in Violet's direction.

Her heart thumped. Since Reggie had come to town, her life had turned interesting like never before. He was completely different from other fellows she knew, especially those who roomed at her mother's boarding house. Reggie made her feel special, and every day was a new experience. Now, he was eager to take her sailing in his uncle's eighteen-foot sloop. She had sailed plenty of times on Sac Bay in a smaller dinghy with Guy, but the prospect of going out with Reggie lent a dimension of excitement to the venture.

"*Please*, Celina!" Violet pleaded. "It will be a great way to pass the afternoon. Reggie won't let you get wet, I'm sure!"

He raised his right hand, palm out. "Not a drop shall splash upon you, Miss Legard. I give you my word!"

With one last glance at the toes of her impeccable boots,

she replied with reluctance. "All right. But you'd better be careful to keep that promise!"

"You'll stay dry as dust!" Reggie assured her.

Within minutes they had cast off, raised the mainsail, and headed out along the bluff on a broad reach. Reggie tied off the sail. His hand rested lightly on the tiller and his countenance sported a confident smile.

Violet turned to her friend. "Isn't this pleasant, Celina? And to think you were worried about getting wet!"

"We'll see what happens when we get farther out," she replied skeptically.

Once past the limestone bluff, the wind took on new energy with waves to match. The boat began to heel to the port side and water splashed over the bow several feet forward of Celina. She nevertheless complained. "You're too close to the wind, Reggie. You're going to get me wet! Fall off the wind and level the boat!"

Reggie immediately adjusted to port, let the sail out some, and again tied off the line. "How's that, Miss Legard?"

"Better, thank you."

No sooner had she spoken, than the wind switched direction.

The boom slammed to starboard.

The boat tipped hard.

Violet and Celina scrambled for the high side.

"We're going over!" Violet warned.

"I'll spoil my new boots!" Celina cried.

The sail hit the water, quickly followed by both girls.

Reggie remained dry, hustling over the starboard side to the centerboard. "Ladies! Get off the sail! Grab the gunwale!" he ordered, attempting to stand on the centerboard and right the boat.

Violet and Celina kicked and thrashed against the sail, driving it deeper into the water until the boat floated bottom side up.

Reggie lay prone on the hull. "Forget the gunwale, ladies! Give me your hands!"

Violet and Celina exchanged mischievous glances, grabbed Reggie, and pulled with all their might.

Reggie met the water with a splash.

Violet and Celina laughed heartily.

Reggie surfaced beside them, his expression one of profound dismay. "Why did you have to go and do that?"

"Serves you right," Celina exclaimed, reaching for the beret that had escaped her head and floated nearby.

Violet chuckled, her gaze on Reggie. "You didn't really think we'd let you get out of this dry, did you?"

"I suppose not." He sighed.

Violet rescued Reggie's straw hat from the waves that threatened to carry it away, then set it on his wet head. "I don't suppose there's any hope of righting the boat now that the mast is pointing straight toward bottom."

He shook his head. "I'm afraid we're dead in the water, in an upside down way."

Celina scowled. "Some commodore you turned out to be! My boots are ruined! Papa is going to have my hide because of you! And look at this dress! Agnes will never speak to me again!"

"I'm so sorry, Miss Legard! Please don't fret. I'll buy you a new dress and boots to match!"

"I don't believe you!"

"I said I would, and I will! But first we've got to get back on dry land."

Violet said, "I hope someone comes along to help us soon, or we'll be out here floating in the waves while everyone else is eating a delicious dinner and kicking up their heels at the leap year dance."

"Oh!" cried Celina. "I'd nearly forgotten! Chase is meeting me at the dance! I've got to be there!" She glanced toward shore, a half-mile off and getting farther away by the minute.

Reggie spoke sternly. "Don't you even *consider* swimming toward shore. The wind and waves are against you, not to mention the weight of that dress and boots. We all must stay with the boat. Soon someone will rescue us, and we'll all be ashore in plenty of time for dinner and the dance. Guaranteed! Now I'll get up on the hull and pull you two up. We'll be on dry land before you know it!"

Violet silently prayed that Reggie was right and they would all be at the dance, but an hour and a half later, chilled to the bone by the increasingly brisk and cool off-shore wind, she couldn't ignore the sinking feeling that washed over her.

On the tug, Jo Harris.

Guy was standing inside the cabin, watching the shore-line as the tug passed South River Bay several miles south of Van's Harbor when Rascal, the terrier mascot, jumped down from his perch on a stool in the cabin, scrambled to the bow deck, and began to bark excitedly.

The captain reached for his binoculars. "Rascal has a good eye for debris. Saved me many a collision with float-ing logs. I always take him serious when he gets out there and sounds his alarm." Raising the glasses, he took a long look, then passed them to Guy. "Tell me what you see."

Guy adjusted the focus on an object between the shore-line and Snake Island. "Looks to me like the wind got the best of three poor sailors."

The captain nodded. "I usually run outside the island, but I think we'd better take the inside route this time."

Minutes later, when the tug was but a few yards away from the overturned craft, Guy stood on deck ready to toss a line. Then two familiar voices called out.

"I'd know that beret anywhere!" Violet claimed.

"It's Guy!" Celina cried.

"Violet, Celina, what happened?" Guy demanded.

Celina quickly explained. "Reggie, here, got caught in a wind shift, and before we knew it, we were in the water."

With the tug now alongside the sailors, Guy tossed the line to Reggie. "Hold fast while I get the ladies aboard."

"Aye, aye, sir!" Reggie replied.

Guy hauled up Violet, then Celina, both shivering from head to toe. "Go inside the cabin. Maybe the captain has a blanket for you."

Guy turned his attention to Reggie. "Are you a good swimmer? Can you dive down and tie the line around the mast?"

"Yes, sir!" Reggie replied, sliding off the hull and disappearing below the surface.

After a worrisome wait, Guy began to wonder if he was going to have to jump in and rescue Reggie. Then the fellow's head popped above the surface, his voice strong and confident. "She's secure, sir!"

Guy nodded, consulted briefly with the captain, and then instructed Reggie. "We're going to back off. When the sail comes even with the surface, stand on the centerboard, hang onto the main sheet, and lean back."

"Yes, sir!"

Slowly the tug eased the mast and sail to the surface. Reggie pulled himself up onto the centerboard, main sheet in hand. Guy reached down, grabbed the top of the mast and pulled up. Swiftly, the sail broke free of the water, righting the boat and sending Reggie into the bay.

Reggie surfaced in an instant and crawled over the gunwale into the water-laden hull.

Guy pulled the sailboat close and handed Reggie a bilge pump. "Drop the sail, cleat the line to your bow, then pump while we tow you in."

"Much obliged, sir!" Reggie began tying off exactly as told.

Guy stepped inside the already crowded cabin where his sister and Violet huddled together in the only woolen blanket the captain had to offer. Torn between his pleasure at seeing them again, and his anger over the dangerous situation in which he had discovered them, he demanded to know, "Who is this Reggie fellow?"

Violet, troubled by her unexpected encounter with Guy, replied boldly. "He's my new friend, Reggie Vanderveen. He's visiting his aunt and uncle at Fayette for the summer. He's a right fine eastern fellow, by jolly, and he knows how to keep me laughing!"

"Except for now!" Celina pointed out. "Reggie's a fool, and so am I for letting you two convince me to go out with you." To Guy, she said, "I thought it would be all right because Reggie was the commodore of the Yale Yacht Club. He promised not to get a drop of water on me. But look! This costume I borrowed from Agnes is soaked, and these boots Papa just bought me are spoiled! I was all ready to meet Chase at the leap year dance tonight. Now, I have to miss out on all the fun!"

Violet countered. "You'll do no such thing! Reggie will buy you a new dress and boots from the Company Store. You and Chase and Reggie and I will have a fine time at the dance tonight, I promise!"

Guy spoke sternly. "Hush! It was no sure thing that either of you would have lived long enough to attend that dance if Rascal hadn't seen you and barked! You'd better thank him and the captain and God almighty that things are no worse!" He turned and headed to the aft deck, muttering into the offshore breeze, "Silly girls! How could they be so foolish?" Then his gaze fell on Reggie in the sailboat. He cut a fine figure despite being soaked to the bone. Guy could tell that this university fellow was used to having his way, especially with the ladies, and Violet had fallen victim. Guy decided to have a talk with the Yale commodore the minute they reached shore.

In the cabin, Violet asked Celina, "Did you know Guy was coming back today?"

"I had no idea," her friend replied. "His last letter arrived a month ago saying he was working at Van's Harbor for a spell. Don't you remember? I showed it to you at the time."

"I remember." Violet sighed. "He goes away for the better part of a year and now all of a sudden he's back and acting like nothing's changed!" To the captain, she said, "Sir, could you tell me, please, what time it is?"

He pulled his watch from his pocket. "A half past three."

"Thank you," Violet replied, her attention again on Celina. "See? We have plenty of time for you to get a new dress and boots for dinner and the dance. You'll meet Chase just as you planned, and it will be like this sailing fiasco never happened!"

"Until Agnes and Papa find out," Celina reminded her.

"Reggie will make things right. If he doesn't, I'll never speak to him again!"

"Some loss that will be. You've only known him for a

week," Celina reminded her.

"He made you a promise and I'll hold him to it, or I don't deserve to be a debater in the Literary Society," Violet asserted.

Celina offered a look of uncertainty.

In the harbor, Guy cast off the line to the sailboat, freeing Reggie to row to shore. A few minutes later, after he helped Violet onto the dock, she turned to him. "We're all having dinner at Grandma's at six tonight—Celina, Reggie, and I. Will you be there?"

"Is that an invitation?" Guy asked.

"As you wish. I won't debate the issue," Violet replied unconcerned.

"I'll be there," Guy firmly declared.

To Celina, Violet said, "We must go and see Reggie right now."

Guy watched them head for the Vanderveen fellow on the other side of the harbor where he was tying off the sailboat. Then Guy turned his attention to the captain and the offloading of his lumber. When arrangements had been made, he went to have some words of his own with Mr. Vanderveen.

Thankfully, the girls had already turned toward home by the time Guy arrived at the opposite side of the harbor. When Reggie saw him, he quickly added a couple of half hitches to the bow line then stepped on shore, his smile sincere and his words congenial. "I want to thank you for your help, old chap! You sure got me out of a pickle!" He extended his hand.

Guy ignored the gesture, his warning stern. "Don't you *ever* take my sister or my friend out in a sailboat again. *Comprends-tu?* Do you understand?"

"Je comprends. I understand."

"Good. I'll see you at dinner tonight." With a modest smile and a hasty handshake, Guy turned on his heel, his steps brisk on a path to the Company Office. As he prepared to bargain hard for the parcel of land next to his brother, Louis's, he couldn't help thinking that the evening ahead was about to present an even more challenging set of negotiations.

Chapter

10

When Violet and Celina had concluded their conversation with Reggie, they went to Grandma's Maple Room—the one where Violet's great-grandmother used to live. They had shed their damp clothes and were towel drying their hair when the door off the kitchen opened and Grandma entered carrying a stack of boxes. Blackie followed close behind.

"The Company Store just sent these things over," Grandma explained. "The three larger ones have Celina's name on them, and the two smaller ones are for Violet and me." She set the parcels on the bed. Blackie quickly jumped up to inspect.

In a flurry, lids were cast aside and tissue folded back. Celina gasped so sharply, Violet and Grandma ignored their parcels to see what was the matter.

Celina spoke with unbridled enthusiasm. "Look at this! Just look!" She held up a russet gown with teardrop jet and grosgrain ribbon trim, and then pressed it against herself and stood before the mirror. "I can't believe it! I never thought …"

Violet finished her friend's sentence. "… that Reggie would keep his promise? I told you he would! You're going to look nothing short of gorgeous, Celina!"

Grandma offered a smile of approval. "Violet is right,

Celina. You'll be the belle of the ball tonight!"

Violet pointed to Celina's other two boxes. "And look! Here are all the undergarments, and a pair of matching cloth boots! I don't see how your father and sister could be angry with you *now*."

Celina grinned and shook her head. "They'll probably thank me for being stupid enough to go out with a fellow who couldn't sail!" Laying the dress aside, she asked, "What did you two receive?"

Violet lifted a bouquet of yellow silk roses—a symbol of friendship—from her box, along with a hand-written note. She read. "'I am a hundred times sorry for the boating accident. I pray we can still be friends. Most sincerely yours, Reginald Vanderveen.'"

Grandma said, "The boy certainly knows how to smooth rough waters. Look at what he sent me!" She tilted her open box for the girls to see.

"Chocolates!" they cried.

Grandma nodded. "Not just *any* chocolates. These are cherry cordials, the finest sweets available in town." Unfolding the note that accompanied her gift, she read. "'I beg your forgiveness for the difficulties concerning Violet and Celina this afternoon. I pray you will overlook my reprehensible actions and allow me to dine at your table as planned. Regretfully, Reginald Vanderveen.'"

Celina said, "That fellow may not be a sailor, but he sure has a way with words."

Violet began searching amongst the tissues of Celina's three cartons finding a folded card, which she offered to her friend. "I just knew Reggie must have written you a note. What does it say?"

Celina read it silently first, then aloud. "'My dear Miss Legard, words cannot express my regret at the difficulties and discomfort I caused you today. I pray—nay *beg* you to forgive me and to accept these gifts as replacements for your damaged costume. Should anything be unsatisfactory in fit or taste, please feel free to return to the store and make exchanges for items of your size and preference. Most humbly, Reginald Vanderveen.'"

Grandma smiled. "Like I said, Mr. Vanderveen has a real skill for calming troubled waters. Now, you'd better try on your costume right away. If need be, I'm sure Violet will be happy to go to the store for you. Meanwhile, I'd better get back to work. It will be dinner time before we know it!" She covered her box of chocolates and then retreated with her gift and Blackie to the kitchen.

When the door had closed behind her, Violet turned to her friend. "Now let me help you into those things. I can hardly wait to see how you'll look!"

A little later, when Celina had donned the chemise, corset, corset cover, petticoats, gown, stockings, and boots that Reggie had sent, she again stood in front of the mirror. Head moving slowly from side to side, she remained silent and unsmiling.

"What is it, Celina? What's wrong?"

Celina suddenly burst into laughter, her eyes dancing. "What's wrong is that *there isn't anything wrong!* Tell me. How could a man—any man—but especially *that* man know my size and preferences?"

Violet shrugged. "He told me he has a sister our age."

"That must be it," Celina allowed. Then she laughed again. "I still don't like your friend, but I sure do like his taste! Now you'd better let me help you get ready."

While Violet dressed, the delicious aroma of Grandma's freshly baked taffy tarts reminded her that dinner would be not only tasty, but also tricky, requiring the ultimate in tact with both Reggie and Guy as her guests. She had finished putting on her best gown and was tending to her hair with Celina's help when Grandpa came home from work, entering through the back door and pausing in the Maple Room.

He blinked once, twice, three times, and then ran a hand through his thin gray hair. "For a moment I thought I was in the wrong house. I recognize this room, but who are these two beautiful young ladies?"

Violet laughed. "Grandpa, you're such a tease! Now go and get ready for dinner. Guests are coming. Later, we're all going to the dance, remember?"

He nodded and passed through to the kitchen.

A few minutes later, Violet and Celina headed to the dining room to arrange the place settings for tonight's special meal, words of anticipation dominating their conversation as they worked.

Finished with business at the Company Office and satisfied that a good bargain had been struck, Guy returned to the dock to check on the unloaded lumber and pick up his bag from the tug. When all seemed in order, he headed to the hotel to stash his bag, and then to the boardinghouse up the hill to pay a call on Violet's mother. Lavinia and Rose would be very busy preparing dinner for a dozen or so boarders, but Guy would be brief, doing his best to gain Lavinia's approval for an interesting plan.

When his brief conversation with Lavinia and Rose had come to a successful conclusion, Guy returned to the hotel to dress for dinner. He was painfully aware that his gray woolen sack coat and pants would never measure up to the fine furnishings that Reggie Vanderveen would wear, but he prayed that Violet was not so besotted with the Easterner that she had forgotten a simple truth—clothes don't make the man.

A few minutes before six, he stood in front of the mirror. Taking a deep breath, he squared his shoulders, put on a smile, and headed out the door. He had taken no more than three strides in the direction of the McAdams home when, to his chagrin, Reggie Vanderveen fell into step beside him carrying a bouquet of flowers.

The doorbell rang just as Violet and Celina finished pouring water into the glasses on the dining table. Violet's heart skipped a beat and she turned to her friend. "You go. If it's Reggie, he'll see how wonderful you look in the costume he sent over. If it's your brother, it would be better for you to greet him first."

While Celina headed for the door, Violet went to the front parlor. Sitting gingerly on a balloon back chair, she heard Celina say, "Guy, Reggie, come in!"

Reggie greeted her with enthusiasm. "Miss Legard, you look lovely as a rose in your new costume! Here, I've brought some tulips and daffodils for Violet's grandmother."

Celina said, "How thoughtful of you. I'll take them to her. Won't you two come into the parlor?"

Violet took a deep breath and put on a smile. Reggie entered the room first with Guy one step behind. Immediately, the differences in the two were apparent. Reggie sported a smart four-button cutaway jacket with a white shirt and narrow tie that showed his trim figure to good advantage and gave him a cosmopolitan appearance. Guy wore a more casual sack suit that she had seen many times before, but tonight it fit more closely than she remembered. Guy's winter of hard labor had added a new layer of firm muscle to his form, making him no less handsome than Reggie.

Violet greeted them both with all the sweetness she could muster. "Reggie, Guy, so glad you're both here!"

Reggie came straight to her, lifting her hand to his lips for a kiss and then holding it while he spoke. "My, but you're looking divine this evening, Violet. Your gown becomes you so, and matches your name as well. How symbolic and tasteful, the very essence of modesty as defined by the language of flowers." He gave her hand a squeeze and then stepped aside to sit on a chair to her right.

For a brief instant, Guy wanted to bash that flowery-mouthed Easterner in the face! Squelching the flare of resentment inside, he paused to take in the picture of love-liness that met his eyes. Violet wore a deep purple dress that he had never seen before. Its matching stripes of velvet trim flowed fashionably down one side of her bodice to a waist so narrow he was sure it would fit within his hands. Suppressing the urge to test that measurement, he placed his palms gently on her shoulders and bent to kiss her ever so softly on the forehead. "Mr. Vanderveen speaks the truth, *ma petite amie*. You are lovely, a soothing sight for eyes accustomed to gazing upon stacks of timber and lumber."

Her smile widened. "Thank you, Guy."

He detected a nervous quiver in her voice and prayed that he would not say or do anything to add to the strain.

Violet sensed the tension in the air and was struggling for the right words to dispel it when Celina returned to announce dinner. At the table, the foursome sat across from one another, Guy and Celina on one side facing Reggie and Violet on the other, with Grandma and Grandpa in their cus-tomary places at either end.

Grandpa offered a prayer. "We thank thee, Lord, for the safety of the young people at our table this evening—Mr. Vanderveen, Violet, and Celina ashore after their sailing mishap, and Guy returning from his work at lumbering and milling. We thank thee, too, for the bounty we are about to receive. Bless the hands that prepared this meal and those who are about to partake of its goodness. In Jesus' name, Amen."

"Amen," echoed around the table.

Grandpa uncovered a platter and took up a meat fork and carving knife. The delicious aroma of cinnamon raisin sauce over pork loin piqued Violet's appetite while he cut a few thin slices for each of the dinner plates stacked in front of him. Within minutes the peas and the fluffy mashed potatoes had been served and all began to eat.

Reggie was the first to assess the meal. "Mrs. McAdams, I do wish that my mother's cook could learn to prepare pork loin with such skill. Your roast is done to per-fection, your sauce is incomparable, your potatoes are smooth as silk, and the peas are *sans* wrinkles. I commend you!"

Guy quickly followed up. "I could not have said it bet-ter myself. Excellent!"

Reggie replied. "You just *did* say it better, old chap, in one word. Excellent!"

Guy bridled at the label, "old chap", but let it pass for now.

Grandma smiled. "Thank you, both. Now let me hear from each of you about yourselves. Reggie, I understand that you were a student at Yale. What did you study there?"

A mischievous smile tilted his mouth. "Nothing much, which is why they sent me packing six months ago. Father was none too happy to see me home, as you could well imagine. He immediately sent me off to John Inglis's ship-yard on the East River in Brooklyn. There, I assisted with the task of constructing the *Eleanor*, a 53-foot yacht com-missioned by Inspector Williams of New York. We launched her exactly three weeks ago and I am proud to say she floated like a cork!"

Grandpa said, "Congratulations on your success, son! Your father must have been pleased."

Reggie nodded. "He was, but as soon as I returned home to Boston, he had a new plan for me. He had arranged for me to spend the summer here with Uncle Horace and Aunt Lottie."

Grandma said, "They're lovely people. I hope you're enjoying your stay."

"I'd be a fool not to, with such fabulous scenery on which to feast the eye."

Violet said, "The bluff in the harbor *is* impressive."

Reggie's gaze settled on her. "The bluff? I was refer-ring to the young ladies!"

Guy wanted to kick the fellow for the way he was open-ly admiring Violet. Then he had the audacity to turn his gaze on Celina. When his sister smiled in return, he tapped her on the ankle a little too hard.

"Ow! Stop it, Guy!"

He was so humiliated he wanted to crawl under the table like a little mouse and up the leg of that Vanderveen rascal.

Violet's grandmother was quick to save the moment. "Tell us Guy, about what you've been doing since we saw you last fall. I understand you worked in the woods until April, and then at the sawmill in Van's Harbor."

"Yes, ma'am. That is the sum of it, six days of hard work and Sunday to rest."

Grandpa asked, "Will you work with your father and

older brothers making charcoal for the J.I.C. this summer?" He referred to the Jackson Iron Company that owned the town. Guy's father had operated a charcoal-making business under contract to the company since the family's arrival on the Garden Peninsula twenty years earlier.

Guy shook his head. "I have a job clearing stumps on a 40-acre parcel north of town." Unwilling to say more on the topic, he offered a question. "Did I smell taffy tarts when I came through the door this evening?"

Grandma said, "Indeed, you did!"

"Then I shall look forward to them after second helpings of the meat and vegetables, and some words from Violet about herself since I left the area last year."

"I, too, worked hard," Violet responded. "Only I didn't get a seventh day of rest. After church services, Mama and Rose and I served dinner to a dozen hungry men. In the boardinghouse business, there is never a day off unless special arrangements are made."

Reggie said, "Couldn't you bribe your younger sister to do the work, like you did today?"

Violet laughed. "As it is, I already owe her a week off from helping with the dinner dishes. I'll be working dawn to bedtime all next week just to repay my debt."

Reggie said, "What a shame. I had hoped we could see one another each evening. I'll be in desperate need of pleasant company after the work Uncle Horace has planned for me. He's secured a position for me twelve hours a day at the casting house."

Guy smiled and tucked into another forkful of pork loin. The hot, heavy job of casting molten iron into pigs couldn't have fallen to a more deserving fellow. Days of hard work and nights of bone-weary fatigue were just what Reggie needed to keep him out of trouble.

Conversation continued on the topic of life in Fayette, followed by Violet's inquiries about living in Boston. Guy could see that Violet was impressed as she listened to Reggie's description.

"There is always something to keep us entertained. Aside from the dinner parties and balls that the young people get up, there are plays, concerts, lectures, and debates. Not an evening goes by without some sort of social or cultural offering. During the day, museums and art galleries, volunteer work, and shopping in the finest of department stores keep the fair ladies of the city occupied."

Violet focused on her friend. "Imagine that, Celina! Always somewhere pleasant to go, and something fun to do!"

Celina said, "How do the ladies get their work done?"

Reggie said, "They have hired help—cooks, maids, gardeners, nannies, and chauffeurs."

Grandma said, "Only a few families here have hired help, and then it is usually one woman who does the cooking, cleaning, and watching the children if need be."

"A maid of all work can be found in nearly all the middle class homes of Boston," Reggie stated. "The wealthier families hire additional help."

Grandpa said, "This remote little town of five hundred must be quite a shock for a fellow as cosmopolitan as you."

Reggie nodded and then turned to Violet with a question. "Have you ever been to a large city?"

She shook her head.

He continued. "You and your friend, Celina should come to Boston for a visit. You could travel East with my Aunt Lottie and me at the end of the summer. My grandmother on Mother's side has several empty bedrooms where you can stay along with my Aunt Lottie. It's only a few blocks from Mother and Father's. While you're in Boston, my sister and her fiancé and I will show you two ladies a very good time!"

Guy could see interest sparking in the eyes of both Violet and Celina, and hastened to quell it. "Such a journey would be far too costly for Celina and Violet."

Celina turned to her brother. "How do you know? Do you know what it costs?"

Violet followed up. "Even if it *is* expensive, who's to say Celina and I couldn't earn our way?"

Guy laughed. "If you started this very minute, it would take you *years* to earn passage to and from Boston!"

Reggie said, "Perhaps not, old chap. I can arrange for their passage if they agree to take positions as domestics once they arrive."

The suggestion ignited Guy's inner fury. The very thought that Celina and Violet should move halfway across the country to a city where they had no acquaintances excepting this rascal, Reggie, was too absurd for words. He bit his tongue to keep his opinion in check, only to be shocked by the calm inquiries that Grandma put forth.

"Who would hire them? People that you know personally? I wouldn't want Violet or Celina unfairly overworked or otherwise mistreated by unscrupulous employers."

"I can assure you that I would allow none but the most reputable of households to hire either Violet or Celina." To Violet he said, "Perhaps you will find a position with a family that travels abroad. Then you can see Europe at your employer's expense." To Celina, he said, "Or maybe the family who hires you will have a summer home at Martha's Vineyard—that's at the seashore—and you can spend your free time sailing a dinghy on the ocean."

Violet's thoughts soared. "Doesn't it sound exciting,

Celina? Think of it! Life in a big city and perhaps trips to Europe or the seaside all in exchange for work that we're doing now for free!"

Celina said, "As long as Reggie isn't sailing the dinghy, I'd be willing to go!"

Guy said, "Surely Mama and Papa will never let you." To Violet he said, "Nor will your mother be willing to give you leave when she depends on your help to keep her boardinghouse operating."

Violet set her jaw. "In a week's time, Rose will graduate from the eighth grade and she is just as capable—even better—than I am at helping Mama with the boardinghouse chores. I'm going to discuss Reggie's suggestion with Mama tomorrow, and then we shall see what she says!" To Grandma, Violet said sweetly, "If you wish, I'll help you clear dinner dishes and serve the taffy tarts now. We could use a little sugar after all this talk about moving to Boston."

Grandma smiled. "You're right, dear. It is time to bring out the dessert."

When the ladies had disappeared into the kitchen Grandpa inquired further of Reggie about the means of obtaining a domestic position in Boston.

The young man replied. "Newspaper notices, word of mouth, and employment agencies are the usual methods of finding good help. Most often, immigrants are hired, but Violet and Celina, being enterprising young Americans, would have an advantage. They should obtain references from their ministers and schools and anyone they have worked for recently. If they haven't been employed outside their homes, each of them should write a careful letter about their work experiences in the area of domestic chores. They also will need three personal letters of recommendation from folks who aren't related to them. About a month before I return to Boston, I will send the girls' credentials to my mother and ask her to look into the prospects for employment. I'm certain suitable posts can be found."

Guy kept silent, his outlook darkened by all this talk of domestic positions out East. The possibility that Violet and his sister would move to Boston had soured his stomach so much that an entire batch of taffy tarts could not sweeten it!

Chapter

11

In the kitchen, Violet chatted excitedly while she helped her grandmother and Celina put whipped cream on the tarts. "Just think of it, Celina, working in a large, beautiful home all day, going to Europe or the seaside all summer, seeing places we've never seen and meeting folks we've never met. Doesn't it sound fascinating?" Blackie circled her feet and meowed as if in agreement.

Celina laughed. "Blackie seems to think so. And even *I* am beginning to forget the trouble Reggie has caused and dream about city life, the seashore, and countries across the ocean."

Grandma set the last dessert plate on the tray and gazed into the eyes of each of her helpers. "Girls, remember. Domestic positions require hard work and long hours. You won't have much time for fun."

Violet laughed. "You just described my life *here*, Grandma. I'm willing to work just as hard in Boston and get paid for it!"

Celina nodded. "At least we will have our own money."

Grandma said, "But you'll be far away from your kin. Won't you be homesick? I know I'll miss both of you terribly if you move away."

Violet offered a quick hug. "I'll miss you, too, Grandma, but I promise I'll write and tell you everything."

Celina remained silent, her expression contemplative.

Grandma picked up the tray. "We'll talk more about this later. It's time for dessert. Celina, would you please pour the tea while Violet helps me serve the tarts?"

With a nod, she picked up the teapot and followed Violet and her grandmother into the dining room.

Violet served Reggie first. "I hope you like this taffy tart. It's a family recipe passed down from my great-grandmother to my grandmother to my mother and then to me."

"I'm sure it is delicious, coming from such a long line of distinguished women," Reggie replied. When all had been served and he had taken a sizable bite, he nodded approval. "This is more than delicious. It is absolutely scrumptious! Is the recipe a family secret?"

Grandma replied. "Goodness, no. It's a simple recipe made of common ingredients found in every pantry. It's not the least bit difficult to bake. Any woman who knows how to make pie crust can do it."

Reggie said, "Except my mother's cook. She's been known to burn water!"

Violet laughed. "Surely you exaggerate."

Reggie shook his head. "Come to Boston. You'll see!"

"I plan to do that!" Violet replied with confidence.

Guy took a sizeable bite of tart, fighting desperately the urge to announce his plan for a home of their own on the forty acres he would clear. Now was not the time to press the matter. He said nothing more until dinner had ended and he had adjourned to the parlor with Violet's grandfather and Reggie while the ladies cleared the table and cleaned up in the kitchen.

There, to Guy's surprise, conversation turned quite pleasant with Reggie's interesting inquiries about the business of logging and milling lumber, and his descriptions of the textile and fishing industries on the East Coast. He turned out to be even more knowledgeable about the sporting life, hunting in the Maine woods for big game, the coastal waters for fowl, and trapping lobsters for family consumption.

When the ladies joined them, conversation turned to experiences of recent years. Taking Blackie onto her lap, Violet stroked the purring feline as she spoke poignantly about the loss of her father and the difficult move to Fayette three years earlier. She made no secret of the importance of Guy and Celina's friendship in helping her through that sorrowful time, and Guy found a lump forming in his throat as he heard her recount the trials of her past.

Reggie proved to be a sympathetic listener. "I'm so very sorry about the loss of your father, Violet. I can't imagine how difficult that must have been. I can tell from the way you describe him that he was a very hard working and loving man, devoted to his family. How tragic that he isn't here today to see what a lovely young lady you have turned out to be."

After a brief pause, Reggie's countenance brightened. "Now, if you'll tell me, Violet, I'd like to hear about the happiest time of your life."

Guy prayed she would name the husking bee. He certainly counted it as his most cherished memory, getting through a rough winter and spring on recollections of that evening together. It gave purpose to his hard labor miles from the girl he adored. But he should have known that Violet's response would be very different.

Following a thoughtful moment, she smiled brightly at Reggie. "My happiest time has been this past week since you arrived!"

Guy's heart fell. Then anger rose within. He couldn't understand how the girl he had watched over from infancy could so quickly turn her attention to such an irresponsible rogue.

Reggie responded to Violet's high compliment with modesty and grace. "I'm honored that you would make such a reply! But I must warn you not to expect too much. As today has proved, I am quite flawed—notorious for seeking out good times, landing in trouble, and avoiding work when possible. Father, bless his heart, is attempting to correct my deficiencies."

Celina said, "God bless your father!"

Reggie chuckled. "I believe God is doing just that. Father sent Uncle Horace strict instructions that starting five o'clock Monday morning I am to labor twelve hours a day, seven days a week at the furnace. Uncle Horace has secured a position for me at the casting house. So I must enjoy this evening as much as possible!"

Guy silently thanked God for the wise plan of Reggie's father, praying that it would keep the troublesome young man too busy and tired to spend time with Violet. But tonight was another matter.

The mantle clock chimed, reminding all that the dance in the Town Hall would soon begin. Guy couldn't avoid the pang of jealousy when Reggie stepped out of the house with Violet on his arm. The grace of his steps, the way he rested his hand over hers, and the inclining of his head in her direction when she spoke, marked him a man of great charisma the likes of which Guy had not seen in these parts.

Guy tried not to think of it, delivering Celina to the Town Hall where Chase was already busy fiddling a welcoming tune before the first dance. Guy hastily excused himself, passing Violet's grandparents on his way out.

Angus rested a hand on Guy's shoulder. "Leaving so soon, son?"

Mary said, "You'll miss all the fun!"

Guy shook his head and smiled. "I'll be back!"

Violet was so busy introducing Reggie to other young ladies of the village that she didn't know Guy had left until she saw him coming through the door with a very familiar figure on his arm. Excusing herself and Reggie, she hastened to greet the woman by Guy's side.

"Mama! I didn't know you were planning to come to the dance tonight!"

Her mother's face lit with the becoming smile she had almost always worn when Violet was young, but which had been seldom seen in the past three years.

Violet embraced her briefly and then parted to admire the blue bodice and pink skirt she wore. The hues were far brighter than anything her mother had donned since becoming a widow. Though a bit behind the times in style, the fit and color combination suited her perfectly, setting off her trim figure to best advantage and making her look far younger than a middle-aged mother of three.

"Mama, you look absolutely wonderful! Where did you get that costume?"

"I borrowed it from your Aunt Flora. Goodness knows she's in no shape to wear it tonight." She referred to her sister's figure being large with child again.

"Very becoming," Violet said brightly, and then turned to Reggie. "Don't you agree?"

"Without a doubt! She is the queen of the dance, and you, Violet, are the princess!"

Violet hastened to ask, "Then you won't mind dancing with Mama just before the last dance?"

Reggie beamed. "I would be honored!"

Violet turned to Guy. "How did you get Mama to agree to come? In the three years we've lived here, she's avoided occasions such as this."

Guy said, "I asked her, and she said 'yes.'"

Her mother explained. "I did it for Guy. I wanted him to enjoy his return to Fayette after such a long absence. No point in him missing the fun just because you had already made plans with Reggie."

To Guy, Violet said, "Thank you for bringing Mama! I'm so glad she's here! Now, if you'll excuse us, we must find a few more partners for the dances."

Guy said, "Wait a moment! You will save a dance for me, won't you, *ma petite amie?* The reel?"

Reggie answered for her. "Of course she will dance the reel with you! See you later, old chap." To Violet, he said, "Do you suppose Celina would agree to be my partner for the reel?"

Violet caught the frown on Guy's face. To Reggie, she said brightly, "I don't know, but I think there's a fair chance if you go and ask her right now."

A moment later, when they found Celina, Reggie said, "My dear Miss Legard, I pray you will do me the honor of dancing the reel with me tonight—if you have not already promised someone else, that is."

"I haven't promised anyone," Celina cautiously replied. "Nor will I promise *you*, unless you can assure me that you are much better at dancing than you are at sailing!"

Reggie chuckled. "Of that you can be certain, Miss Legard! But even if I am not, you would only be risking a bruised toe, not a dunking."

"All right, then, the reel is yours. But don't you dare step on these new boots!"

With the strains of the first dance, a waltz, beginning to play, Reggie turned to Violet and took her into his arms, stepping off with a grace unequalled on the Town Hall floor.

Violet felt as though she was being swept off her feet, and she was keenly aware that her friends were admiring her partner and eager for their turns with him on the dance floor. Around and around they went, every move fluid, every step perfectly timed. Violet caught herself daydreaming, imagining that instead of the Town Hall, she was in the third floor ballroom of a mansion in Boston, a room decorated by swags and streamers and swirling with beautifully gowned young ladies held in the arms of perfectly groomed young gentlemen. So vivid was the scene that when the music ended, she needed a moment to clear it from her mind and return her thoughts to the less glamorous reality of Fayette.

The next several dances passed quickly as she partnered with furnace workers from her mother's boardinghouse and other young men that worked at the Company Store, the stock barn, the hotel, and the Carpenter Shop. When the musicians paused for a few minutes' break, her last partner saw her off the dance floor, leaving her in her mother's company.

Chase had set down his violin and was headed for Celina when Guy interrupted him. Their brief exchange ended with a nod by Chase and a turn in direction by Guy to take up the idle violin and bow. Soon, the lively strains of *Gary Owen*, a folk song that had been among her parents' favorites, drifted over the hum of conversations taking place at the edges of the empty dance floor.

Before Violet knew it, her mother's feet were moving. She lifted her skirt for the heel-toe steps of the jig the way she had many times at their home in Sac Bay. William Burley, a dark-haired, broad-shouldered teamster of her mother's generation, noticed and began dancing too, his hands at his thick waist. The two of them stepped in time to the music, circling one another. Chase and Celina joined them, along with Grandma and Grandpa.

Reggie took Violet by the hand and led her onto the dance floor, saying, "Teach me the jig!"

Lifting her skirt, Violet showed him the heel-toe steps, which he mimicked perfectly, until the end of the dance. No sooner had *Gary Owen* come to an end, than the strains of *The Galway Piper* rang out. With little persuasion William Burley kept Lavinia on the dance floor. While others stepped back to watch and catch their breath, Violet's mother seemed to be more energized than ever.

Reggie started clapping in time to the music. Violet joined in, and then others until the tune could barely be heard above the sound of their happy hands. The simple steps of the jig became more complex, with William squatting down and extending his legs in front of him, alternating to the time of the rhythm. Then, with his hands on the floor, he kicked his legs out behind. Jumping to his feet, he kicked his legs high, touching his toes at waist height. Then he took Lavinia by the hand and spun her beneath his arm once, twice, three times.

She wobbled.

Violet's heart skipped a beat.

Instantly William's muscular arm went securely about her mother's slim waist and they heel-toed their way off the dance floor to loud applause, whistles, and shouts of approval. Willilam, his blue eyes sparkling, bowed deeply to her mother, backed away, and then turned to join his friends on the opposite side of the hall.

Violet hurried to her mother. Her cheeks were red as cherries. She pressed her hand to her midriff, all the while trying to catch her breath, but the smile on her face beamed happiness beyond any Violet had seen since her father's passing.

"Mama, are you all right?"

"I'm … better than all right … I'm delightfully, delectably, deliriously tired!" She pulled a handkerchief from her sleeve and blotted moisture from her forehead. "I'm going to have to get in shape if I'm ever to keep up with William Burley."

Violet smiled despite her reservations about the tough and rough-spoken Irish teamster who boarded on the third floor of the hotel with the roughest of the furnacemen.

Reggie stepped near. "Mrs. Harrigan, did I not tell you that you would be the queen of the dance tonight? Well done! Now rest. I can't have you overtired when my turn comes to take you out on the dance floor." He pulled a chair up for her.

"Thank you, Reggie. You needn't worry. I'll be well-recovered by the time our music is played."

Indeed, her mother sat resting while Violet danced with various partners for the polka and gallop. Then the Virginia Reel was called and lines formed. Violet's grandmother and grandfather headed the line and her mother and William stood beside them. Guy ushered Violet to the third place in line and then Celina and Reggie joined them. Two other couples completed their line and the dance began.

"Honor your partner!"

Chase struck up *Durang's Hornpipe* just as he had when Violet and Guy were at the barn dance last fall. The music put a smile on Violet's face, but Guy's appeared strained. When the calls went out, he performed his part perfectly, but he did not look like he was enjoying himself. Stiffly, he went through the motions. His mind seemed to be elsewhere. Then, when he and Violet reached the head of the line, he suddenly offered her a bright smile, took her hands firmly in his, and gracefully sidestepped down the center

99

and back.

Guy's attention remained keen on Violet while the last two couples took their turns at the head of the line. When the reel ended and a fox trot was announced, Guy's arm went tightly about Violet's waist and he swiftly ushered her toward the door.

Violet resisted. "Where are you taking me, Guy?"

"Outside. I have something to say to you." He spoke quietly but insistently.

"Why can't you say it here?"

"It is private."

"Then wait until some other time. I don't want to leave the dance now! Reggie will—"

"He will not mind in the least if I spend a moment with you," Guy said confidently. He gazed deep into her eyes, his tone softening. "Please, *ma petite amie*. Do this one thing for me."

Reluctantly, Violet went with him.

Outside, the velvety sky sparkled with diamonds in the cool of the night. Guy held her close while guiding her to a spot a few yards away. There, near the dimly lit dock, he pointed in the distance to the silhouetted stack of some sort of freight.

"Do you see that? It is lumber. *My* lumber," he said proudly. "I am going to build a house."

Violet opened her mouth to ask questions, but before she could get a word out, Guy continued.

"I put half down on the forty acres next to Louis's today. I am going to clear stumps for a farm and a farmhouse."

She remembered that at dinner he had said he was going to work this summer clearing stumps. She was more surprised than ever to learn that the stumps were on his very own land.

He turned to face her and gazed deep into her dark eyes. "It is for us, *ma petite amie*. This fall I will go into the woods again. By spring I will have the money to pay off the land. Then I will work at the sawmill in Van's Harbor long enough to get the lumber for a barn—a couple of months at most. I will come home and plant and put up my barn. In fall, I will sell my crop and go into the woods, and in spring to the lumberyard. Then I can afford to marry you. Promise me, Violet Harrigan that you will be my wife."

Violet's heart skipped a beat. Her mind raced. She shook her head and pushed free.

"No! Oh, no, Guy! We are *friends*, that is all."

"Do you not love me? You *know* that you do!" He stepped near and reached for her.

Again, she moved away. "Yes, I love you, Guy, like a *brother!*" Anger rushed past affection, spilling out in a flood of words. "Last fall, after the husking bee, I thought there was more between us. I fell in love with you that night. I thought you loved me, too, then you left. For nine months I heard nothing of you except what Celina could tell me. You broke my heart, Guy!" Struggling to keep tears in check, she spun around and hurried toward the Town Hall.

Guy followed and caught her by the arm. Turning her toward him, he spoke in earnest. "Forgive me, *ma petite amie*. I did not mean to hurt you. I had to leave. Do you understand?"

She gazed up into eyes so full of compassion she nearly fell in love with him all over again. But those days were gone. "I understand," she said coldly. "I understand that you have a plan for us and that you want me to promise to be part of it. Well understand this, Guy. I have a plan of my own. The end of this summer will by *my* time to leave. I am leaving Fayette and going East to taste the life that Reggie described, and I expect Celina will go, too."

Guy's jaw hardened, his grip tightening. "I forbid you, Violet. I forbid Celina, too. That Vanderveen fellow has no more substance than the puff of wind that overturned his sailboat!"

"How do you know? And how dare you forbid Celina or me from doing what we want? Now, let me go!" Wrenching free from his grip, she lifted her skirt and headed for the Town Hall.

Guy watched her, his heart going with her. Then he turned and stormed toward the pile of lumber that was to be his house—*their home*—on the forty acres he had yet to clear. Raising his fist, he slammed it down on the top board and then kicked the pile with his toe. Without Violet, his plans had no meaning. The wood could rot where it lay.

Turning toward the Town Hall, he could hear the strains of the last waltz beginning to play. He owed this one to Violet's mother since he had escorted her to the dance. Quickening his pace, he hurried into the hall to find Lavinia sitting with William, enjoying a friendly chat. Celina sat with them, her gaze on Chase who stood with his musician friends at the end of the hall playing a moving rendition of the Blue Danube.

The moment Lavinia caught sight of Guy, she smiled and beckoned. When he offered his arm to lead her onto the dance floor, she made a different suggestion.

"Guy, I beg you to excuse me from this dance, and I have another favor to ask of you. Your sister, here, has had very little time this evening with her good friend, Chase. Would you please escort her to him, take his place with the ensemble, and finish playing this lovely waltz so that the two of them can have this last dance?"

"Of course, I will be happy to do so." Guy placed

Celina's hand on his arm and led her to Chase, who was more than pleased with the suggestion Lavinia had made.

Guy took the violin in hand and began to play. Then his gaze fell on Violet. She moved across the floor as one with Reggie, her face beaming. They talked as they danced, and though Guy could not hear the words exchanged, he was certain they were making plans to go East together at the end of the summer.

Guy played with all the passion he could muster, wondering all the while how he would convince that headstrong young lady to change her mind about leaving Fayette.

Chapter

12

Six weeks later
Friday afternoon, July 27, 1888

Sweat poured off Guy's face as he set the stick of dynamite in the stump and began laying the fuse. When he was several feet away, he lit the fuse and ran as fast as he could.
Boom!
Guy hit the ground and covered his head with his arms. A few seconds later, he rose and returned to where the stump had been. A small crater was all that remained. Root debris and topsoil littered a wide area. He wasn't sure if dynamite was the best method of clearing a field for planting but it didn't require a team of horses, which he could not afford to buy or rent. He had hoped to borrow his father's team, but with the two furnaces at Fayette in blast, they were too busy hauling charcoal.

Before resorting to dynamite, Guy had spent weeks attempting to rid the stumps by burning them, but they smoldered endlessly and the roots beneath the surface remained a problem still. He prayed he would be able to effectively fill the craters left by the explosions, and moved on to set another charge.

The third stump had gone up in smoke when Guy saw a horse and rider approaching in the distance. The horse was white with large dark markings like none he had seen in the area, and at first he assumed the rider was a young boy curious about the loud blasts. But as the visitor drew near, he realized that his unexpected guest was a female in blue jeans riding astride a mare without a saddle.

She appeared to be about his age. Her wide-set hazel eyes sparkled, lit by the smile of her generous mouth. Dark tresses shimmered in the bright sun and fell in cascades upon the shoulders of a blue plaid shirt. Her evident disregard for hats had resulted in a tan that seemed to enhance her natural beauty rather than detract from it, as was the prevailing notion. When she greeted him, her voice was low and melodic.

"Hello, there! I'm Mattie Silverstone, your neighbor to the north. Couldn't help hearing your blasts. Had to come and see what they were all about."

"Clearing my forty, is all," Guy replied with a smile.

Shading her eyes with her hand, she scanned the stump-riddled field, taking notice of the three depressions at the center. "Loud and fast, that's your method, I see. More power to you, Mr. ...?"

"Legard, Guy Legard."

Mattie focused on him. "Glad to make your acquaintance, Mr. Legard. Now I'll get out of your way and leave you to your work. Good day!"

Guy tipped his hat, then watched as she turned and headed off, going from trot to canter to full gallop. He had set off a half-dozen more charges when he again caught sight of Mattie on her horse. This time, she came bearing a brown jug.

A friendly smile preceded her neighborly words. "It's a mighty hot day. Thought you could use something cold to wet your whistle." She offered him the jug, explaining, "It's just lemonade, but it does the job. I don't believe in firewater."

Guy took the jug in hand, pulled off the cork, and tipped it for a long draught of the icy beverage. He could tell that the lemons had just been squeezed. It was neither too sweet nor too sour, but perfect for quenching his powerful thirst. When the jug was half empty, he pressed the cork in place and handed it up to her. *"Merci beaucoup.* You're very kind."

"You keep it. You'll need it. I'll come by just before suppertime for the jug." She paused. "Better yet, I'll come by for you *and* the jug. Ma's a real fine cook. After supper you can ride with us over to the Town Hall dance. Got to try out that new maple floor they laid there, ya know." She turned her mount to go."

"Miss Silverstone, wait!"

She paused to look back.

"Thank you for your kind offers, but I must decline."

A rueful smile tilted her mouth. "Sorry to hear that. Can't blame a girl for trying, can you?" In an instant, she was off.

Guy returned to his task, but his heart wasn't in it. He had heard about the dance the last time he went to town, but had forgotten about it until Mattie brought it up. He had gone to Fayette for supplies once a week since the last dance. Each time, he had stopped by to see Violet, and each time, she had been polite, but cool. The moment he tried to reason with her against going East, she would end the conversation by telling him she must return to her boarding-house chores. This week, she had dismissed him by saying she must complete a description of her work experience. She was preparing to send it off to Reggie's mother along with several personal references by the end of the week.

As for the dance tonight, Guy assumed Violet would

attend with Reggie. The thought irked him and it troubled him that his presence there would not be welcomed by her any more than his calls had been over the past six weeks. For a moment he considered taking Mattie up on her invitation. At least she would appreciate him.

He dismissed the notion as quickly as it came. No point in wrongly raising hopes in Mattie only to see whether Violet would come his way. He doubted the scheme would work, anyhow.

Setting a stick of dynamite into another stump, he lay the fuse, lit it, and ran, stumbling over a root and falling hard to the ground a few short of his goal. Hands over his head, he waited for the blast. A moment after the explosion, a heavy chunk of stump landed on his right shoulder.

The pain was excruciating and at first he thought his shoulder might be broken. Slowly, he tried rotating it, succeeding despite the pain. Thankful that he had suffered only a bad bruise, he called it quits for the day, put the lid on the crate of dynamite, and started walking toward his brother, Louis's place where he had been staying. He knew Louis had a large block of ice in his icebox for a cold pack. While his brother and just about everyone else hereabouts went to try out the new maple floor in the Town Hall, Guy would be sitting home alone nursing his shoulder.

Five weeks later
Saturday, September 1, 1888

Boom!
Guy got to his feet and headed to the crate for another stick of dynamite, and then paused. In the distance, Mattie was approaching on horseback. Since their first meeting weeks ago, hardly a day had passed that she had not come

by with some liquid refreshment and pleasant conversation. When she noticed him favoring his injured shoulder, she had brought horse liniment to ease the swelling and pain. Thankfully, he had healed almost completely.

Guy wished he could say the same thing about his relationship with Violet. He had continued to see her weekly, but she remained cool with him. How he had prayed that she would greet him with a bright smile the way Mattie always did, but that prayer had gone unanswered. He would have been quick to blame the Vanderveen fellow if not for Celina. According to her, Reggie's time and effort was being poured into the casting house job leaving him too drained for socializing. Guy silently thanked God for that. Then he gazed up to return the smile that his neighbor was now offering.

"Hey, there, Mr. Legard, time for a break, don't ya think?" Mattie handed down a jug.

Guy nodded, smiled, and began to drink.

Meanwhile, Mattie slid off her mount, dug with the toe of her boot around a chunk of limestone, then worked it free and carried it across the field to where rocks had been piled along a fence line.

By the time she returned, Guy had corked the jug. "Thanks, for your lemonade and your rock hauling, neighbor."

"My pleasure!" Mattie's height, equal to his own, allowed her to gaze directly into his eyes. "Come for supper tonight?"

Guy was expecting the question. She had never failed to ask it. Before he could decline, she went on.

"Seems to me it's about time you accepted my invitation. I'd think by now you'd be worn out with my asking."

Guy had been careful to limit his contact with Mattie to

these casual daily encounters. Today, he had good reason for turning down yet another invitation to supper.

"Thanks for your kind offer, but again I must refuse. I'm going to Fayette for supper tonight, a farewell supper. My youngest sister and a good friend, someone I've known since birth, are heading to Boston to work as domestics."

Mattie's smile dimmed and he could tell that she was turning over his words in her mind. After a moment, she said thoughtfully, "I think I understand now why you never come to supper. Good day, Mr. Legard." She took her half-empty jug from his hand, mounted her horse, and rode off without ever looking back.

Guy watched her go with mixed feelings. He knew that since she had taken her jug, she had no intention of returning. He would miss her visits, but this was best. His loyalty still belonged to Violet and he didn't want Mattie to think otherwise.

He gazed up into the overcast sky. A bright spot marked the place where the sun was trying to shine through, but clouds were casting a thick shadow over the day and within his heart as well. Perhaps both would clear by evening. He prayed it would be so. Starting toward the crate of dynamite, he decided to set off one more charge and then head to his brother's for a bath. Afterward, he'd have just enough time to see the barber at Fayette for a haircut and shave before supper.

Chapter

13

Dressed in the lavender shirtwaist and black skirt that Violet had carefully chosen for her trip, she carried a bucketful of fried chicken in one hand and a basketful of biscuits in the other. Celina, wearing a white shirtwaist and dark brown skirt, walked beside her carrying a tray full of taffy tarts, sugar cookies, and apple turnovers. The hum of conversation and occasional shouts of small children rose up to greet them as they descended the hill to the center of town where tables had already been set for their farewell dinner.

Violet spoke excitedly. "Can you believe the number of people who have come to see us off? I thought Mama was crazy when she insisted that the backyard was too small."

Celina chuckled. "Your mama's backyard is *far* too small. In my family alone there are fifteen including my folks, my brothers and sisters, and their little ones."

"They'll be easy to count," Violet observed. "The black berets and that Stetson perched atop Louis' head will stand out in any crowd this far from Quebec."

Celina nodded. "Add to them your own kin—your Uncle Toby and Aunt Elin and their three children who came all the way from Wisconsin to surprise you—plus your grandmother and grandfather, your brother and sister, and your Aunt Flora, Uncle Sven, and their four children. And then there are Reggie and his aunt and uncle."

"You didn't mention the twelve men from Mama's

boardinghouse who have to be fed," Violet added.

"We've named almost fifty people, not counting friends like Chase, and your neighbors here in the village," Celina concluded.

Passing the Town Hall and entering the village green, Violet was surprised at the number of people who had gathered since her previous trip down the hill to set places for her family and Celina. "There must be a hundred people here now, don't you think?"

"At least!" Celina replied, finding a place for the dessert tray on the end of the long food table. Taking the basket of biscuits from Violet, she helped her friend find room for them and the bucket of chicken at the opposite end of the table.

Violet thanked her and continued. "Once word had spread about the supper, it seems everyone in town wanted to join in."

Celina said, "I think folks want their share of your grandma's tarts, turnovers, and cookies."

Violet laughed. "Don't say that too loud. Reggie has been working hard on his fish boil, claiming it's the best anyone in Fayette will ever taste. At least that's what I heard him saying to Mr. Burley a couple of hours ago." She gazed in the direction of the shoreline where Reggie and several men had gathered around the huge pot.

"That Reggie is so full of himself!"

Violet turned to her friend, seeing the spark of her words reflected in her blue eyes. "Reggie may be high on himself, but not without cause. He's worked very hard every day at the casting house all summer long. According to Grandpa, that fact has not gone unnoticed by his bosses. He's never missed a day, or even an hour!" Violet paused, remembering one more point. "His father didn't think he could do it, but Reggie proved that he *is* responsible and trustworthy."

"You've nearly convinced me, champion debater that you are!" Celina laughed. Then, glancing to the north, she said, "I see Louis coming down the hill over there. I thought Guy would be with him. I wonder—"

"There's Guy, coming out of the Barber Shop."

"And here come Dan and Joseph!" Celina pointed to the road that entered from the south.

"I'm so glad Mr. Richbourg loaned them his wagon." Violet named the farmer a few miles south of town for whom the boys had been working all summer while living in the loft of his barn.

Celina said, "I don't see Chase. He was supposed to catch a ride with them. I wonder what happened."

While the boys parked the wagon, Reggie's Aunt Lottie approached the girls with a bowl of fresh melon. "Do you ladies suppose there's room for this on the table?"

"Of course!" Violet assured her. She was making space for the melon when she saw that Celina had gone to greet their brothers, and that Joseph was handing her a folded slip of paper. Setting the melon in place, she thanked Aunt Lottie and joined Celina, who was studying the missive. "What is it, Celina?"

She looked up, the sparkle gone from her blue eyes. "Chase isn't coming. He says he was offered a chance to play for a party at Fairport tonight for good pay." She named the village at the southern end of the Garden Peninsula. "Can you believe it?"

"I'm so sorry!" Violet replied.

"I am *so angry!*" Celina's voice broke, and a tear slipped down her cheek.

Violet handed her a handkerchief and slipped her arm about her friend.

Just then, Reggie approached. Learning of Celina's situation, he said tenderly, "I know you're disappointed that Chase won't be here to sit beside you at dinner and to see you off. But look on the bright side. Now, you get to sit next to me!"

Celina dried her tears, the spark returning to her blue eyes. "You're no help! All I wanted was this time to say good-by. All summer, Chase has been busy playing his violin for money, with almost no time for me. Couldn't he have put me first just this once?" Spinning around, she hurried away.

Reggie followed after her. Violet would have, too, but her Aunt Elin and her cousin, Ingrid, who was now seven years old, interrupted.

Elin said, "Ingrid has something to give you." To her daughter, she said, "Show Violet what you've made for her."

Ingrid pulled a small piece of fabric from her pocket, unfolded it, and held it up for Violet to see. "This is for you, Cousin Violet. I hope you like it!" Her smile reached from one blonde braid to the other.

Violet took the handkerchief from Ingrid and ran her fingers over the violet blossom in the corner. "How beautiful, Ingrid! You've done a fine piece of embroidery, and I see you've hemmed the edges very nicely, too. Thank you! Whenever I use this, I will think of you! You'll write to me in Boston, won't you?"

Ingrid nodded.

Violet stooped to kiss the little girl's cheek. "You're so sweet! Now, are you hungry? It's nearly time to eat."

Again, Ingrid nodded, and then went with her mother to find their places at one of the long tables.

As Guy watched Violet moving toward Reggie and

Celina near the head table, jealousy and melancholy stabbed at his heart. He was wondering how he might still turn the tide on her leaving when a new situation captured his attention.

Coming down the road from the north was the unmistakable piebald mare belonging to Mattie, but the rider was sidesaddle, not astride. Swiftly, he headed toward them, wondering who it might be. He almost didn't recognize Mattie in her stylish riding habit and tall hat. Her bodice clung closely to her curving, corseted form and a bustle accented her backside. The toes of her shiny boots peaked from beneath the hem of a draped skirt that cascaded in gentle folds to cover her ankles. The picture she presented was so pretty that he almost forgot the awkwardness her presence imposed.

Mattie spoke first. "I had to see for myself the reason why you never come to supper. Who is she? The pretty dark-haired one?" She referred to Celina.

Just then, Violet caught sight of them and started toward them.

Mattie grinned. "It's the redheaded spitfire, a tad jealous and coming to check on you, isn't it?"

Guy replied with a slight nod.

"She looks mighty young, not really a woman yet," Mattie observed.

Violet didn't wait for introductions. "Hello! I'm Violet Harrigan, Guy's friend. And you are?"

"Miss Mattie Silverstone. Guy and I are neighbors."

Violet reached up to shake Mattie's hand. She pulled off her riding glove and offered a firm grip.

Violet continued. "Pleased to meet you, Miss Silverstone. You're just in time for my farewell dinner. You're welcome to stay."

A tense moment passed and then Mattie smiled and shook her head. "Thank you kindly, Miss Harrigan, but I have chores to do before dark, so I must get home. Good evening!" She swung her horse around and trotted out the way she'd come.

Violet turned to Guy. "She must be new in these parts. I don't believe I've ever seen that piebald mare in town or I surely would have remembered it. How long has she been your neighbor?"

Before Guy could answer, the dinner bell rang. He offered his arm. "I'll see you to the head table."

After a moment's hesitation, Violet smiled and placed her hand in the crook of his arm, aware now of the clean lemon-like scent of the barbershop hair tonic. She wished Guy hadn't gone to the trouble and expense of a fresh hair-cut and shave on her account. On the other hand, he *did* look more handsome tonight than he had all summer long with his neatly trimmed mustache, his clean-shaven chin, his perfectly combed hair, and deep brown tan.

When they reached her place, Guy held her chair. Then he went to find his own place with his mother, father, brothers, and sisters halfway down one of the long tables that was set perpendicular to the head table. Glancing back at Violet, it bothered him that she and his sister sat either side of that East Coast fellow who had started all this trouble a little over two months ago. The thought of the girls leaving later this evening put a knot in his stomach and killed his appetite. But he would not put a damper on the event for everyone else.

With a smile on his face and pleasant words from his mouth, he tucked into a piece of whitefish as if nothing was amiss. He even admitted that Reggie Vanderveen knew a thing or two about how to boil fish. He was sure no one could guess that deep inside, his heart was breaking with every moment that brought Violet's departure closer.

When dinner was nearly over, Angus McAdams stood to offer good wishes to Violet, Celina, and Reggie. While he spoke, Guy organized his last argument against the girls leaving. The trick would be to find a moment alone with them to make his case. Reluctant as he was to renew strife among them during their last few hours in Fayette, it was his one final chance to salvage his plans for a future with Violet.

Then Violet stood to make a farewell speech.

"Thank you all for coming to say good-by." She held no notes, yet appeared calm and confident, presumably due to her many public speaking experiences as a debater in the Literary Society. She gazed out across the audience and smiled. "I am grateful for your good wishes and thankful that you have been my friends and neighbors for the past three years.

"Many of you know that when I first moved to Fayette, my family was in deep mourning over the loss of my beloved father. You welcomed us and made us feel at home. We had been here only a little while when some neighbors and relatives decided to move to Wisconsin. This evening reminds me of that time. It was in September, and a farewell dinner even bigger than this one was held. Some of you remember it, I'm sure.

"At that dinner, I listened to some words from a wise gentleman named Lars Lindberg. He said, 'Vhether in the State of Michigan or the State of Visconsin, I vill be all right.'" Her audience chuckled at her imitation of his accent.

She continued. "I remember wondering at the time if I would ever have as much faith as Lars did about moving.

Now, that day has arrived and I know the answer. So with thanks to Mr. Lindberg for the lesson he taught me, I can say to you, whether in the State of Michigan or the State of Massachusetts, I will be all right. Thank you, and farewell."

Violet sat down to a round of applause and whistles. Soon a crowd of friends and neighbors surrounded her. Guy watched from a distance. Eventually, the well-wishers cleared away and Violet and Celina returned to the buffet table where they picked up a basket, bucket, and tray. When they headed up Stewart Avenue, he hurried after them, over-hearing a few words of their conversation. To his delight, Violet was asking Celina what she knew about Mattie. He was sure of what her answer would be, since he had never mentioned Mattie to anyone, but before a reply could be made, he spoke up.

"Let me carry that basket and bucket for you, Violet."

She whirled around. "Guy! I didn't know you were behind us. I was just asking Celina about your neighbor, but I might as well ask you. How long has she been living on the peninsula? I'd never seen her before tonight."

Guy shrugged and changed the topic. "Do you need help getting your trunk down to the dock? I'll be glad to bring Papa's wagon up to get it."

"Thanks, but, no. Reggie came earlier to haul it down for me. I'm going inside to freshen up and pack a few last essentials in the carpetbag I'll carry with me on the boat and train."

"I'll wait and carry it down for you," Guy offered.

"No need. I can carry it."

"I know, but it would be my pleasure to do this one last favor. Won't you allow me, *ma petite amie?*" Guy smiled hopefully.

After a moment's thought, she returned the smile.

117

"Sure. If you insist, you may carry it." Resuming her conversation with Celina, they chatted excitedly about their trip until they reached the McAdams home. Blackie greeted them with a hungry "meow." Setting bucket, basket, and tray in the kitchen, they made sure to seclude Blackie in the Maple Room with a bowl of milk so she wouldn't tamper with the leftover food. Then they went next door to the boardinghouse to freshen up while Guy sat on the porch step and waited.

While they were inside, Guy's head swam with all that he wanted to say to Violet, and the arguments he had already made to both her and his sister. In these moments alone, he realized that there was no point in resurrecting the old conflict. He would offer a few words of caution, carefully delivered. That much was his duty as a friend and older brother.

When the girls emerged, Guy took the carpetbag from Violet and said, "I'd like to have a few words with you both, *s'il vous plaît.*"

Celina offered a quick reply. "If you think you can keep us from leaving—"

"I know I cannot do that," Guy swiftly admitted, "but I am worried. After you get to Boston, you might soon wish you were back here again." He set down the carpetbag and turned to Violet. "There are many things about Reggie that you do not know, and that you might discover later to be unacceptable. But by then, you will be a thousand miles from home with no way to get back."

Violet sighed. "Guy, I've known you all my life. Even so, I was not expecting you to leave town, to leave me the moment I fell in love with you." She paused, stopped by the lump that was forming in her throat and the unexpected surge of emotion that came flooding into her heart.

Determined to keep her voice from breaking, she continued. "I was not expecting my heart to be broken by the one who had been protecting me for all of the years that I was growing up."

Guy heard the pain in her voice and saw the moisture in her brown eyes and wished desperately that he could erase it, but what was done, was done. "I never meant for you to be so hurt, *ma petite amie*. I can only pray that you will forgive me someday." He reached for her hand but she drew back.

"I have forgiven you, Guy, and I have learned." Steeliness edged her words. "It doesn't really matter that I haven't known Reggie all my life. It's what I *do* know about him that counts. He is no longer the foolish fellow of the past, but reliable and hard working. Now, he has a good job waiting for him at the Quincy Shipyard. He's going to be successful, and I'll be right there to see it."

Guy turned to Celina. "Perhaps it is good that you are going, too. At least one of us will be there with Violet when things don't turn out the way she planned."

"How can you know that?" Celina challenged. "We're going to have a jolly time. We will have jobs with respectable families, and Reggie has promised that there are many nice fellows in Boston who would love to meet me. They are bound to be more interesting than Chase, who would rather be playing his violin in Fairport than spending time with me on my last night here!" To Violet, she said, "We'd better go. A lot of relatives are waiting to say goodby to us."

Guy said, "You go, Celina." He pulled a piece of folded purple velvet from his pocket. "I have something to give to Violet, and then we will be right along."

Celina hesitated until Violet said, "Go ahead. I'll be

119

there in a minute."

When Celina's footsteps had faded, Guy reached for Violet's hand, grasping it securely in his strong, rough one. "We have been friends for a very long time, *ma petite amie.*"

He spoke quietly, reverently, and when she looked up, he captured her in his tender, blue-eyed gaze—the one that she had seen hundreds of times since she had been a very small girl. Memories of her childhood in Sac Bay flooded over her. Hunting for morel mushrooms, gathering trillium bouquets, picking thimbleberries, losing her beloved father.

Guy's firm squeeze of her hand brought her back to Fayette and the present. His voice grew husky. "I love you, *ma petite amie.* I will always love you, no matter what. Please accept this as a token of my affection." He pressed the folded velvet into her palm.

With trembling fingers she carefully opened it to discover a necklace—a stunning cloisonné violet blossom on a purple satin ribbon. She had never seen a pendant so lovely, so perfect, and so appropriate. A tear threatened to spill down her cheek. Swallowing past the knot in her throat, she asked, "Will you put it on me?"

He nodded, and though it took him a minute or two to tie the ribbon properly with his callused fingers, he finally managed to fasten it about her neck so that it hung perfectly between the two rows of lavender lace on her bodice.

She gazed down, taking it in her hand to study it for a moment. Then, she turned it over, discovering an engraving on the backside. It said, "*Je t'aime.* I love you." Without aforethought, she flung her arms about his neck and hugged him fiercely.

Guy held her tight, hope rising as he whispered in her ear. "It is not too late to change your mind and stay."

She pulled back, a determined look darkening her brown eyes. "I will not change my mind, but I have something important to say to you." Her gaze softened. "I am sorry for the trouble between us these last couple of months. I was wrong to be so difficult. I pray you will forgive me."

He nodded and tried to pull her close again, but she stepped free. "It's time for me to go. There are so many people I must bid good-by before the *C.W. Moore* arrives." She started toward town at a brisk pace.

Guy picked up her carpetbag and followed her. On the village green, friends, neighbors, and boarders from her mother's boardinghouse offered words of encouragement and prophecies of success. Violet responded with handshakes and hugs and a large dose of enthusiasm for her new adventure.

Daylight turned to dusk, and too soon Violet heard Reggie say, "The steamer's coming!"

Mixed feelings stirred within. Excitement for her future fought with deep affection for her family and her dear friend, Guy. Surrounded by those who loved her most, she made her way dockside.

Violet offered parting words to her grandparents and her Wisconsin kin, and then Mr. Burley approached. Taking her hand in his, he kissed it and held it while he offered words that were all too familiar.

"May the sun shine warm and a gentle breeze blow, and until we meet again, may God hold you in the hollow of His hand."

That Irish blessing, spoken exactly as her father had on many occasions, struck a chord within. She struggled for composure. "Thank you ... thank you and God bless you, Mr. Burley!"

With a tear in her eye, she turned to her mother, wrapping her arms about her and hugging her fiercely while her cheeks grew damp and memories of her father flooded her mind.

"There, now," her mother consoled. As if reading her thoughts, she whispered, "If Papa were here, he'd be very proud of the beautiful and confident young lady you've become."

"But … would he want me to go?"

She pulled back and looked Violet straight in the eye. "He never wanted his family to be far from him, but he would have encouraged you to follow your dream, like he did when he was young and came here from Wisconsin. I'm sure he's watching over you this very minute, praying for you to be happy, safe, and successful, just as I am."

The words calmed Violet and offered reassurance. "Thank you, Mama. I love you. Stay well and write often."

"Of course, dear." She kissed Violet's cheek, and then released her.

Dan stepped up. "Don't expect any letters. I'll pray for you, though. Take care." With a hug and a kiss on her cheek, he gave way to their younger sister.

Rose wrapped her arms about Violet and squeezed tight. "I'll sure miss you, Sis!"

"And I, you," Violet replied kissing her cheek. "I know you'll be good and do everything Mama asks."

Rose nodded and brushed a tear from her cheek with the back of her hand.

The captain called out. "All aboard!"

Violet turned to step onto the gangway, halted by a familiar hand on her arm.

Guy held up her carpetbag. "Aren't you forgetting something?"

Violet laughed and took it from him. "Thank you, Guy!

What would I do …" She dared not finish the sentence. Touching a finger to her new pendant, she said, "Thank you. Thank you for everything." With a lump in her throat, she walked up the gangway and onto the deck of the steamer to join Celina, Reggie, and his Aunt Lottie.

Reggie was all smiles as he addressed Violet and Celina. "Well, ladies, we're casting off for your new adventure. You're going to love the Connelly family, and they will love you. So dry your eyes, put on your best smiles, and be happy for what is to come!"

Taking his advice to heart, Violet smiled and waved, hoping to rid herself of the last vestiges of sadness that lingered within. On shore, her family waved fiercely. She looked for Guy among the cluster of Legards but he was not there. As the steamer moved toward the narrow harbor entrance, she spotted him on the spit of land beyond the sawmill.

He waved to her and Celina with a wide sweep of his arm. *"Au revior! Bon voyage!"*

They replied nearly in unison. *"Au revior, Guy!"*

Violet lifted her gaze to the grassy rise behind him. She remembered running up that hill three years ago when her kin had left on this very steamer for Wisconsin. She wondered then, how many others in Fayette would leave to find their fortunes in fairer fields. Tonight, on the other side of the good-byes, she clung to her conviction that this truly was her time to leave.

Chapter

14

December 24, 1889

Violet could hardly wait to see her family again. How grateful she was when the carriage she had boarded in Escanaba finally reached the Garden Peninsula and headed south. After more than a year in the bustling city of Boston, the rural landscape of Upper Michigan seemed tranquil and soothing, and the long ride gave her ample opportunity to reflect on the situation she had temporarily left behind.

Since taking up residence with the Connellys in their Boston mansion, not a day had gone by that she hadn't thanked God for the opportunity to live and work with such a delightful family. Although she had started there as an upstairs maid, her position soon changed to that of nanny to the family's two young children, Patrick age four, and Katherine age two. Violet smiled as she recalled how diligently Patrick worked at learning to play catch, hit a croquet ball through the wickets, or ride his pony at the farm where his pet was boarded. Katherine was completely entertaining, capturing attention with her songs, dances, and charm in the way only a two-year-old can. Violet missed the children already, but soon enough she would return. In a few months' time she would go with them and their parents on an extended trip to Europe where their father would conduct business while the rest of the family visited relatives and took in the sights. She leaned back and closed her eyes, drifting to sleep while the carriage rolled closer to her destination.

Sometime later, she awoke to the see that dusk was already starting to settle over the peninsula. At a little past five o'clock, the carriage pulled into Fayette. The young couple riding with her, newlyweds bound for Sac Bay, chatted excitedly about the Christmas surprise they would share with family when they reached their destination, but Violet's attention was keenly focused on this place she had left a long time ago.

Light snow filled the air, falling gently on the few inches that already covered the ground and settling on cold, dark furnaces and casting houses that had been shut down until spring. Violet's mother had written about the lack of business, idle furnaces, and the necessity of closing up the boardinghouse. She had told, too, of families leaving, including Aunt Flora, Uncle Sven, and their four children who had moved last month to cutover land nearby where they had built a house and barn and would start farming next spring. Even so, the town seemed too quiet. The Machine Shop, Company Store, and Town Hall were dark, with only the hotel showing lights in the windows and signs of activity.

A glimpse of the docks, quiet now that the shipping season was over, reminded her of the night she had left Fayette and of the gift Guy had given her. Since then, not a day had gone by that she hadn't worn the cloisonné pendant, read the inscription on the back, and pondered the depth of its meaning. And not a week had gone by that she hadn't received a letter from Guy confirming his love for her. Silently, she thanked God that over time, she had been able to leave problems of the past behind, fall in love with him all over again, and tell him so in weekly letters of her own. She looked forward to the day that she would be able to tell him of her love in person, but Guy's last letter removed any hope that his boss would give Christmas leave to the men in the woods. As the driver turned up Stewart Avenue, she offered a brief prayer that she would find joy in Christmas even though her heart longed for the one gift she would not receive—time with Guy.

And then her thoughts swiftly returned to the quiet Fayette street as she rode past the dark boardinghouse her mother used to run, and came to a halt in front of her grand-parents' home where everyone would be gathered. The friends who had been riding with her wished her a Merry Christmas, then the driver helped her down from the car-riage, carried her bags to the doorstep, and climbed back up to his seat. She stood there alone, facing the fragrant pine wreath that encircled the doorknocker. Taking a deep breath, she picked it up and began to pound, mimicking the rapid beating of her heart.

Quickly, the door opened to reveal the cheerful faces of her mother and grandmother. With a wave to the driver and her friends, Violet stepped into the warm embrace of the two women she loved most. Tears of joy dampened all three faces while hugs melted away the long separation. When Violet released them to look into their shining faces, she silently thanked God that her mother looked even younger and happier than when she'd last seen her, and her grand-mother showed no signs of aging.

Her private prayer ended when her grandfather, brother, and sister joined the reunion, and demanded hugs of their own. Grandpa held her tight and kissed her cheek, laughing when she teased him about his ever-increasing bald spot.

Dan had grown taller by a couple of inches and more muscular in the shoulders since their last hug. He smiled proudly when Violet made mention of it. Rose, too, had gained a bit in height, yet retained her slim figure. Her freckles had begun to fade and her hair had grown longer. It was tied back at her neck, and cascaded nearly to her waist in thick, attractive waves. She was growing into a lovely young woman and Violet made a point to tell her so, earning a second hug from her cherished sister.

When they parted, Violet noticed William Burley standing a few feet away, smiling cheerfully and cradling Blackie in his arms. The Irishman's rosy cheeks and rounded belly made her think that with a red suit and white hair and beard, he could pass for Old Saint Nick—until his thick brogue dispelled the notion.

"Welcome home, Miss Violet. 'Tis a blessed day, indeed, to see the blush of roses in your cheeks and the sparkle of sunshine in your eyes on this dreary eve."

As if to confirm his words, Blackie meowed softly.

And then a storm of questions blew in.

"How was your trip?"

"How long can you stay?"

"Will you be here for Sven and Flora's tenth anniversary on December twenty-eighth?"

"Wasn't that Celina in the carriage? Who was that furhatted fellow with his arm around her?"

Violet began to laugh. "Before I give answers, I have a question of my own. Which of you strong gentlemen will carry my bags upstairs?"

Dan was quick to grab them. "I'll do it if you promise not to give any answers until I get back!"

"I promise! Thank you, Dan."

Grandma said, "Come into the parlor, everyone.

Lavinia and I will bring hot cider, and we'll all hear what Violet has to say."

She turned for the kitchen, but Violet stopped her with a question. "Grandma, what's that glorious aroma I smell?"

Her mother replied with a proud smile. "William shot a turkey yesterday!"

Rose said, "Grandma made cranberry dressing, Mama baked pumpkin pie, and I made stuffed squash."

Grandpa said, "It's a welcome home feast *and* a Christmas Eve celebration."

Dan came pounding down the stairs, a thick wave of red hair falling across his broad forehead. He shoved it back in place and focused on Violet, his brown eyes sparkling. "Did I miss anything?"

She laughed. "Only a recitation of tonight's menu. Come into the parlor. While Mama and Grandma pour the cider, I'll go upstairs and freshen up. In a few minutes I'll be down to answer all your questions."

Grandpa put his arm about Dan's shoulders. "Come on, son. We'll stoke the parlor stove, light the Christmas tree candles, and bring enough chairs so you won't have to sit on the floor."

When Violet entered the parlor a few minutes later carrying gifts for each member of her family, the beauty of the illuminated tree, the aroma of orange-cinnamon balls, and the fragrance of pine filled her with the joy of the season and memories of Christmases past. She carefully placed her presents under the tree, and then turned to look for an empty chair.

Rose beckoned from one end of the sofa. "Sit here, Sis, between Dan and me."

Violet took the place between her brother and sister and to her surprise, Blackie jumped down from William's lap and up onto hers, purring contentedly.

Her mother handed her a glass of hot cider and allowed her one sip before repeating her earlier question.

"How was your trip?"

"As good as could be expected this time of year, with the crush of holiday travelers and heavy snow causing delays on the rails. The hardest part was finding someone in Escanaba who was willing to drive over here on Christmas Eve. Thankfully, we located a young single fellow with no plans and the ambition to earn some good pay."

Grandma said, "I recognized Celina in the carriage, but who was that fellow? He had his arm around her as if he owned her."

Mama said, "Yes, who was that? At first I thought maybe Chase had gone over to Escanaba to meet her, but it didn't look like Chase."

Violet shook her head. "It wasn't Chase." She paused for a sip of cider, then said, "It was her new husband."

Rose gasped. "Celina got married? When?"

Her mother said, "Why didn't you tell us?"

Violet explained. "The wedding took place a couple of weeks ago. Celina asked me to keep it a secret until she could come home and tell her folks in person."

Grandpa grinned. "They'll be in for a Christmas surprise. I hope they like her present."

Dan said, "Joseph's got himself a new brother-in-law and he didn't even know it. What's the fellow like?"

Violet said, "He's a fine upstanding gentleman from a good family—wealthy, too, I might add."

William laughed. "Luck o' the Irish, that's what I'd say if I didn't know that your friend was French Canadian!"

Lavinia said, "Maybe her husband is Irish."

Violet laughed. "Irish, indeed! Reginald

O'Vanderveen!"

Rose looked puzzled. "Reginald O'Vanderveen? Do you mean—"

Violet nodded. "Reggie Vanderveen!"

Grandpa said, "Celina married Reggie? How do you like that?"

Grandma said, "Hard to believe. They were always at such odds with one another when they were here."

Mama said, "Didn't you write several months ago that Celina had left her position as laundress with the Connelly family and gone to work as the upstairs maid for the Vanderveens?"

"That's right," Violet confirmed. "Soon after, things changed between Celina and Reggie. They bickered like mad at first, but then a new spark kindled between them, a romantic one that burst into flame after they'd been living under the same roof for a while. Before they knew it, they were deeply in love and Reggie was determined to wed her no matter what."

Rose said, "I thought *you* were going to marry Reggie someday."

Violet shook her head. "I was taken with Reggie at first, but soon after I arrived in Boston I realized we would never be more than friends." Touching the cloisonné pendant that Guy had given her, she said, "I love working for the Connelly family and caring for their children, but I don't expect to live the rest of my life in Boston, so far from the ones who are most important to me. Celina seems perfectly suited for it, though, and I couldn't be happier for her!"

Grandma said, "You were at her wedding, I assume."

Violet smiled. "I was the maid of honor. It was the most wonderful wedding and reception ever, and Celina was a beautiful bride!"

Grandma rose. "I want to hear all about it over dinner. It's time to serve up the turkey!"

When all were seated around the dining table, Grandpa asked a blessing. "Almighty Father, we thank thee for the special gift of your Son on this evening when we celebrate His birth. We thank thee for the provisions on this table that will nourish and sustain us. We thank thee for those gathered here from far and near. Now bless this food to our use. In Jesus' name, Amen."

"Amen," echoed around the table.

A few minutes later, when the plump bird had been carved and everyone had received their desired portion of turkey, dressing, gravy, and stuffed squash, conversation returned to the Boston wedding with Grandma asking, "Where were they wed? In Reggie's church?"

Violet shook her head. "In the front parlor. Mrs. Vanderveen had decorated the fireplace mantle and small tables in the corners with lengths of white netting and fresh white roses. Amongst the netting and flowers, she nestled several white pillar candles of various heights. The lit candles and the fire in the fireplace provided soft light for the evening ceremony. The best man and I were the only two outside the immediate family who were in attendance. But the reception was a different matter!

"Afterward we went to the banquet room of one of the finest hotels in the city where a hundred guests were waiting. There was a table piled high with beautifully wrapped wedding gifts, and another table held a three-foot-high wedding cake and a huge punch bowl. An orchestra was playing while we dined on steak and seafood, and then they played dance music and everyone enjoyed themselves immensely until well past midnight."

William said, "'Twas a night to remember, I'm sure, but

not so memorable as an Irish weddin', with jigs bein' danced and a keg o' stout flowin' freely to keep the throat moist and the feet movin'." His blue eyes twinkled.

Violet laughed. "No stout, to be sure, but plenty of wine for those so inclined."

Mama said, "While we're on the subject of weddings, Flora and Sven were married nearly ten years ago. Will you be here for the celebration three days after Christmas? You haven't said how long you can stay."

"I'm not expected in Boston until the fifth of January," Violet explained. "Celina and Reggie and I will all start back on Friday, the third."

Rose said, "You mustn't let on when you see Aunt Flora and Uncle Sven tomorrow, but there's going to be a big surprise party for them at their house on their anniversary."

Violet grew puzzled. "Didn't you tell me in your last letter that Mama was planning to have cake and tea here that afternoon?"

Grandpa chuckled. "Since that little plan, your grandma and mama have gotten together with some of the other ladies around the area, and now it's become a combination anniversary and housewarming party with a big potluck dinner to be held at Sven and Flora's. But they won't know anything about that until they go home from here."

Dan said, "Besides the housewarming, some of the farmers are planning to give Sven equipment for his barn—things he'll need to start up farming next spring. Mr. Richbourg had an old plow that he let Joseph and me fix up. Now, it's good as new."

William said, "I repaired a cultivator that Mr. Mercier had cast off."

Grandpa said, "I collected some leaky buckets that we didn't need here at the furnace and repaired them. Other men are bringing a trough and some mangers."

Rose said, "The ladies have been real busy, too. Mama and Grandma and I have sewn a slipcover for Flora's parlor sofa.

Mama said, "Three other ladies have made curtains for the bedrooms."

Violet said, "But, what can I give them?"

Mama answered. "Your presence. They'll be thrilled that you are home long enough to enjoy their special day."

Violet sighed. "I had something more tangible in mind."

Grandma said, "If you want to make them something useful, I have flour sacks you could hem for kitchen towels. It wouldn't take long and I don't know a woman on earth who couldn't use a few more kitchen towels."

Violet smiled. "Thanks, Grandma! I'll do it the day after Christmas!"

Conversation flowed freely on other topics for the next several minutes. Sliced turkey, gravy, dressing, and stuffed squash made their way around the table a second time, and then Mama served her pumpkin pie laden with generous dollops of whipped cream. All were enjoying the rich, spicy treat, which Violet was certain came from Mrs. Richbourg's own famous recipe, when her mother's conversation took an unexpected turn.

"I suppose this is as good a time as any to make a little announcement." Her gaze and tentative smile took in everyone at the table, then settled on William, who grinned and winked.

Her smile broadened, and then she continued. "William has proposed marriage and I have accepted. We're to wed one week from tonight, on New Year's Eve!"

Grandpa responded with a hearty, "Congratulations, you

two!"

Grandma said, "I'm so happy for the both of you!"

Rose turned to William. "That will make you my papa, won't it?"

Dan hastily replied. "He'll be our stepfather, and a right good one, too!"

Violet said, "I'm so thankful I'll be here for your wedding. Where will you hold the ceremony?"

The betrothed couple exchanged playful glances and then William answered. "We thought it'd be fittin' to wed in the Music Hall, where we danced our first jig together."

Lavinia said, "It will be the first event of a New Year's Eve celebration. We've already hired Chase and a couple of his musician friends to play for a party that night, although they don't know yet that it will begin with a quiet little wedding, just family. We'll invite everyone in town and all who come to Sven and Flora's celebration to join us afterward for a big reception and party." To Violet she said, "Will you stand up for me?"

"Of course, Mama!"

Lavinia turned to Rose. "And will you please be my bridesmaid?"

"Oh, yes, Mama!"

"Wonderful! Now, I have but one more request." She turned to her father. "Papa, will you please give me away?"

"Again?" he asked jokingly. "Of course, daughter. Gladly, in fact!"

When everyone laughed, he quickly added, "Now don't you go and take that the wrong way! I'm not eager to lose a daughter. I'm pleased to be gaining a son!"

Conversation buzzed about the impending nuptials for several minutes after the pumpkin pie had been consumed. When the men retreated to the parlor, Violet helped her grandmother, mother, and sister to clear the table, set a kettle of wassail on the stove to simmer, and wash the dishes.

Talk of the wedding continued, with her mother telling Violet, "My wedding reception will be quite modest in comparison with Celina's, but I expect folks will enjoy themselves. Will Guy be able to come, or will he have to celebrate New Year's Eve at his camp in the woods?"

"He'll be in the woods," Violet quickly replied.

Her grandmother said, "Surely he's home for Christmas. He'll be up to see you sometime tomorrow, I assume?"

Violet shook her head. "Just before I left Boston, I received a letter from Guy saying that none of the men in Guy's camp are being allowed leave for Christmas or New Year's."

Rose spoke up. "How awful! I think I'd just quit if someone told me that!"

Grandma shook her head thoughtfully. "Such a shame. Here you've come all this distance after more than a year away, and now, you won't be allowed to see him at all. It doesn't seem right."

Violet pressed her lips together. Struggling to keep her disappointment in check, she turned to a new topic. "Mama, have you decided on decorations for the Music Hall? How will you make it look like a wedding, *and* like a New Year's Eve party?"

Lavinia's brown eyes lit with enthusiasm. "I've given that lots of thought and here's what I've decided…"

An hour later, with the kitchen work done, Blackie fed, and the wassail warm and fragrant and ready to serve, Violet helped fill a tray with cups of the Christmas beverage and a plate of gingerbread cookies. When she carried it into the parlor, a soft light enveloped her in the holiday charm that filled the room. Small candles flickered on the tree, and one large single candle glowed steadily on the center table, illuminating the Bible that lay open to the Christmas story that Grandpa would read later.

As she moved around the room with the tray, eager hands reached for the refreshments being offered. Conversation turned to the events of the past year, and Grandpa suggested that each person tell what he considered to be the greatest blessing of the past twelve months.

Grandma began. "I'm most thankful for good health. I haven't had any spells or even a single bad day this year, praise be!"

Violet's mother said, "I'm thankful for William's proposal!"

William quickly responded. "And I'm thankful ye accepted!"

Everyone chuckled, and then Grandpa said, "Violet, it's your turn. What was your greatest blessing?"

Violet pondered the question. Scenes flashed through her mind. Being maid of honor at Celina's wedding. Guy's faithful correspondence that reminded her weekly of his love and his plans for their future. Reuniting with her family after the long separation. She spoke thoughtfully. "I've received so many blessings, it's hard to choose. But I suppose if I had to pick just one, it would be—"

The loud, urgent sound of the doorknocker interrupted.

Looks of concern flashed between her grandparents.

Dan sprang to his feet.

Grandpa put up a staying hand. "I'll go, son." Exchanging his worried look for a half-hearted smile, he said, "It's probably one of the neighbors wanting to wish us a happy holiday."

Grandma said, "At this hour? It's nigh unto midnight."

William said, "Me thinks it must be Santa!"

Grandpa responded with a hearty, "Ho, ho, ho," as he closed the parlor door behind him.

All grew quiet, and Violet listened intently, hoping to recognize a familiar voice in response to the welcome that she heard her Grandpa offer, but only Blackie's loud meows were audible.

A moment later, her grandfather opened the parlor door partway, fixed a compelling look on her, and said brusquely, "Violet, come here!"

Chapter

15

Troubled by the urgent request of her grandfather, Violet sprang to her feet and rushed to the hallway. Standing there was a fellow who looked like Guy. She blinked several times wondering if she was imagining things, but when she looked again, he was still there.

"Guy?"

"*Oui, ma petite amie!*" Swiftly, he pulled her into his arms, holding her so tightly that words were not possible.

She wrapped her arms about his neck, taking in the glorious woodsy aroma that permeated his mackinaw jacket. Her throat tightened, and tears welled up and rolled down her cheek, dampening his in the process. In the thrill of the moment, she was somehow aware that her grandfather had scooped up Blackie and retreated behind the parlor's closed door, giving her and Guy complete privacy.

He held her for he didn't know how long, and then he tenderly took her face in his hands, kissing her on the forehead and on each cheek. Fixing her warm brown eyes with his steady gaze, he spoke the words that he had uttered in many a winter dream.

"*Je t'aime, ma petite amie. Joyeux Noël!*"

"I love *you*, Guy! This surely *is* a Merry Christmas!" Tears spilled down her cheeks.

Guy kissed them away with the gentle brush of his mustache. "There, there, *ma petite amie.* All is well. We are together now."

His reassurance helped Violet to gain control of her emotions. She managed a smile, and then gave voice to the question swirling in her head. "How did you get leave from lumber camp? I thought your boss said no one could go home for Christmas."

His expression turned solemn. "He did. Plans changed. The top loader Louis and I worked with nearly got us killed yesterday." He referred to the man who loads logs to a height of ten feet on a sleigh to be hauled from the woods.

She drew a sharp breath. "What happened?"

"The night before last the top loader told us his watch was missing and he wanted it back. We told him we didn't have it. He didn't believe us—said he'd get even. Yesterday morning we all went to the woods as usual. Louis and I kept doing our jobs as 'groundhogs' sending up the logs. Then, last thing in the afternoon, part of a load fell and nearly landed on us. Louis and I scrambled out of the way just in time. It was no accident. This morning my brother and I quit and collected our pay. We've heard there's work at a camp north of the Little Fishdam. We're heading up there the day after New Year's."

"The day after New Year's!" Violet repeated with surprise. "That means you'll be here for Flora and Sven's anniversary, and for New Year's Eve. I can't believe it! Have you been home yet?" she asked, wondering if he knew about Celina and Reggie.

He shook his head. "Louis and I started from camp right after breakfast. We got to Fayette two hours ago. We took a room at the hotel and got hot baths just before I came here. We figure to meet up with the rest of the family tomorrow morning at church and go home with them after services. Celina must be with them now?"

She nodded, and for the briefest moment, considered telling him about Reggie. Then she decided not to spoil this special moment. Thrilled to know that Guy would still be in Fayette come Christmas morning, she hugged him impulsively. Then she hung his mackinaw and beret on the hall tree, took him by the hand, and opened the parlor door.

"Look, everyone! Here's my greatest blessing of the year! Guy has time off until the second of January!"

Grandma said, "Praise be!"

Grandpa said, "That's wonderful news, son!"

Mama said, "Then you'll be here for our wedding!"

Violet explained to Guy. "Mama and Mr. Burley are to be wed in the Music Hall on New Year's Eve. There's a big party afterward. You'll come, won't you?"

"I wouldn't miss it!" Guy replied. "Congratulations to the bride and groom!"

Lavinia beamed. "Thank you, Guy. Now come sit down. I'll bring more wassail and cookies for everyone." To Dan, who occupied one end of the sofa, she said, "Son, please fetch a chair for yourself, and let Guy have your place there next to Violet."

Guy sat close, taking her hand in both of his and holding it possessively until the refreshments were served.

When wassail and gingerbread cookies had made their way around the room, Grandpa said, "Guy, before you arrived, we were each naming our greatest blessing this past year. Violet said hers is having you home from lumber camp for the holidays. What is yours?"

He turned to Violet with a look of overwhelming fondness and quietly answered, "Seeing you again, *ma petite amie*. That is my greatest blessing since you went away."

Her heart danced, and she silently thanked God for the

love in Guy's eyes, and the tenderness of his words.

The conversation about blessings continued with Grandpa naming steady pay in tough times as his greatest blessing. Rose said having Violet home for the holidays was her greatest blessing, and Dan echoed the sentiment.

With the blessings counted and the wassail and gingerbread cookies gone, Grandpa opened the Bible and began to read the Christmas story, starting with the second chapter of Luke.

"'And it came to pass in those days, that there went out a decree…'"

While he read, Violet contemplated the deep love of Joseph for Mary, and their long journey to Bethlehem. She thanked God that He had given the two of them a love strong enough to overcome their difficulties, and prayed that He would bless her and Guy with a similarly strong love to carry them into the future.

"'…And the shepherds returned, glorifying and praising God for all the things that they had heard and seen, as it was told unto them.'" Closing the Bible, Grandpa said, "God bless the reading of His word. Now," he looked around the room, a smile widening, "who wants to open the first present?"

Grandma said, "It's well past midnight, Angus. Maybe we should save our gifts until we've all had a good night's sleep."

A chorus of disagreement rose up including Blackie's anxious meows.

Grandpa said, "A compromise is in order. Each of us will pick one gift to open tonight. We'll unwrap our presents one person at a time, from the youngest to the oldest, so we all can share the joy. Rose, you're first."

She went to the tree and picked out the gift Violet had

brought from Boston. Carefully peeling back the tissue, she revealed a pair of hair combs adorned with silver filigree roses. "Thank you, Sis! I love them!" Rose exclaimed, untying the ribbon from her hair and inserting the new combs that garnered compliments from all.

Dan had also chosen his gift from Violet, a smallish cube-shaped box covered with gold foil and topped with a perky red bow. Instantly, he removed the wrapping, popped off the lid, and emptied the round object into the palm of his hand—a grass- and dirt-stained baseball.

Violet explained. "That ball was pitched by none other than Charles 'Old Hoss' Radbourn of the Boston Beaneaters."

"'Old Hoss' Radbourn?" Dan asked, unbelieving. "Five years ago, he won the National League's pitching Triple Crown. He had a 1.38 ERA, 60 wins, and 441 strike-outs!"

"That's right!" Violet confirmed. "Mr. Connelly caught that ball in the stands this past summer and gave it to me for you."

"Thanks, Sis! Wait till I show this one to the guys on the farm!"

Grandpa said, "Don't use it to practice your catching. You might not get it back!"

Dan nodded and dropped it into its box, admiring it one last time before replacing the lid.

Violet said, "Now, it's my turn to open a gift." She glanced at the presents still stacked beneath the tree. "But which one should I choose?"

Guy answered, "This one." From his shirt pocket, he pulled a narrow box wrapped in red tissue and tied with green satin ribbon.

The shape of the present was the same as the gift she

had chosen for Guy, and she prayed they were not identical. When she had removed the wrappings and opened the lid, she discovered to her delight that her fear was unfounded. Guy's gift was unique and beautiful. Nestled in the velvet-lined box was a stunning silver pen engraved with her name. Around it swirled an intricate pattern of violet blossoms.

"This is gorgeous, Guy! Too nice to use!" She carefully removed it and held it as she would to write.

"You had better use it!" he warned with a smile. "I expect a letter each week, no excuses!"

"No excuses," she promised. She lay the pen in the open box and passed it around the room for others to admire, then retrieved her gift for Guy from among those remaining under the tree.

Admiring the shiny silver foil and matching ribbon that adorned the slender parcel, he asked, "Could it be a pen?"

Violet smiled. "Open and see."

He wasted no time peeling off the ribbon and wrapping. Inside, on a cushion of red velvet, lay a letter opener of scrimshaw etched with his name. He held it up proudly for all to see. "I expect to make frequent use of this at the camp!"

Violet's mother said, "I hope Violet will receive stationery this Christmas. It would be a shame for the pen and letter opener to go wanting for lack of writing paper."

Grandma said, "I think we can remedy that, if there isn't already some stationery waiting for Violet under the tree. Now, Lavinia, it's your turn. Which gift will you choose?"

William answered for her. "This one!" From his pocket he pulled a tiny little box covered with emerald green velvet and placed it in her hand.

"You shouldn't have," she said quietly.

Violet was certain the box contained a ring. With bated breath, she watched her mother pop open the lid.

Lavinia gasped with delight, snapped the box shut, and scolded her husband-to-be. "This is way too precious to you, dear. Are you sure you want me to have it?"

"Aye!" he replied.

Opening the box again, she turned it for all to see. "It's the gold ring worn by his mother from the time she was wed until she was buried."

William said, "I give it with one request. Wear it on your right hand until the day we marry, and then I'll put it on your left hand at our weddin'."

She nodded. Slipping the ring onto her right fourth finger, she held out her hand for all to see.

When Violet saw the shiny, narrow band, a mixture of feelings rose within—happiness that her mother had found someone to love and care for her, and guilt over disloyalty to her father. Her guilt increased when her mother turned to William and kissed him on the cheek. Then, Violet caught a vision of her father looking down and smiling with approval, and all sense of disloyalty vanished.

Grandpa gazed at the ring, his vivid blue eyes and deep voice softening with more than a hint of sentimentality. "That's a real fine gift William has given you, Lavinia. Now, I expect you have something more tangible than a kiss for him tonight?"

"Indeed, I do." Her brown eyes sparkled. From the presents beneath the tree, she chose a very small item wrapped in red tissue and tied with white string. "This will serve you well, I pray."

William turned it over as if inspecting it thoroughly. "It appears that Lavinia and I ascribe to the same philosophy— good things come in small packages." He slipped off the string and peeled away the tissue to reveal a combination knife with a stag horn handle. "Aha! A replacement for the pocketknife I wore out a while back. Only this one looks a good deal fancier." He opened the various items, eleven in all including knives, scissors, a buttonhook, awls, a corkscrew, and a nail file.

Dan said, "That's got even more gadgets than Mr. Richbourg's, and he paid over two dollars for his from Montgomery Ward!"

Grandpa said, "It's a folding tool chest, all right!"

Grandma said, "Now I know who to come to if I can't find what I need. It'll be right there on William's pocketknife!"

He smiled. "I'd be right proud to loan it ye anytime! Now, seems to me you're the next one to open a gift."

Grandma nodded and went to the tree, picking out the present Violet had brought from Boston. Running her hands over the red tissue surfaces and edges, she said, "It has the shape and feel of a book. Violet knows how I love books." Carefully she untied the green ribbon and pushed back the wrapping. A red leather volume emerged with no title on the cover or spine. Grandma opened it to read the inscription inside. "'To my dear Grandma, here are the best recipes from the Connelly household. Add yours to the blank pages so that someday, they will be passed down for the younger generations to enjoy. Love, Violet. December 25, 1889.'" She read the recipe titles. "'Boston Cream Pie, Boston Baked Beans, Boston Brown Bread.'" She chuckled. "I'll be real interested to give these recipes a try. And then I'll put in all the wonderful Michigan and Canadian recipes that are a tradition in this family. Thank you, Violet, for this very thoughtful gift."

"You're welcome, Grandma. Now, be sure to write the

taffy tart recipe in the book, even though we all know it by heart. Someday, your great-great-granddaughters might want to know how they're made."

William said, "And don't forget the cranberry dressing, and the gingerbread, and the wassail."

Guy said, "And the cassoulet."

Grandma nodded. "Of course! Your sister taught me that wonderful recipe of your mother's."

Lavinia said, "Mama, I have a feeling you will be busy writing down recipes for a while. Maybe Violet will loan you her new pen until she goes back to Boston."

Violet said, "I'd be honored to have Grandma write her recipes with my pen." Turning to her grandfather, she said, "Now it's your turn to open a gift. I have something very special for you from out East. Would you like to open it now?"

"I'd like that very much!"

Violet found a small box with a gold foil lid tied with a narrow band of red satin ribbon.

Her grandfather immediately noticed the name embossed on the lid. "Brooks Brothers! They're known for fine men's suits."

Rose immediately spoke up. "I could be wrong, Grandpa, but that box looks too small to hold a suit."

William said, "'Less, o'course, it's for a leprechaun. Ye wouldn't have some Irish magic runnin' in those veins o' yours, would ye? Regular fellow by day, leprechaun come midnight?"

Grandpa's eyes twinkled. "If I did, I wouldn't admit to it!"

Laughter erupted. Then Violet said, "Mr. Connelly picked out my gift for you when he was in New York on business. Brooks Brothers was fresh out of leprechaun suits when he got there, but he hopes you'll like his choice."

Grandpa slipped off the ribbon and the gold foil lid, folded back white tissue, and held up a pair of brown kid gloves trimmed with fur at the wrist. "A very stylish and practical gift! Thank goodness, the leprechaun suits were gone!" He pulled one glove on. "Fleece lined, and a perfect fit! Thank you, Violet! And be sure to thank Mr. Connelly for his excellent selection!"

Grandma said, "Now that we've each opened a gift, I'm turning in."

Grandpa rose. "So am I. Good night, everyone."

Lavinia chased Rose and Dan off to bed upstairs, saw William out, and then went to her quarters in the Maple Room at the back of the house, leaving Violet and Guy in the parlor.

Alone with Violet at last, Guy slipped his arm about her and pulled her close, gazing into the beautiful brown eyes that had appeared in many a lumber camp reverie.

Though fatigued by the strain of the trip and the lateness of the hour, Violet was not too tired to feel the thrill of Guy's nearness.

He spoke quietly. "One last gift I leave with you, *ma petite amie.*" He lowered his lips to hers with a brush of his mustache, offering a brief kiss that threatened to turn into much more. With great restraint, he brought it to an end, stood, and drew her off the sofa. Then he rose, and she saw him to the door.

When he had donned his coat and beret, he took her hands in his. "I'll see you tomorrow, *ma petite amie.*"

"Come for breakfast an hour before church and bring Louis," she suggested.

He nodded, kissed her on the forehead and then took his leave.

Violet hated to see him go, but contented herself with the knowledge that he would soon return, silently thanking God for the unexpected gifts He had already bestowed on her this Christmas. Making sure to extinguish all the candles in the parlor, she carried a lamp to the bedroom she was sharing with Rose. She assumed her sister would be asleep, but when she entered the room, Rose quietly greeted her.

"Merry Christmas, Violet!"

"Merry Christmas, Rose! Now hush. You should be in dreamland." She set the lamp on her dresser and then unfastened her skirt and petticoat.

"I know. But I can't help wondering."

"Wondering what?" Violet asked, removing her shirt waist and corset cover.

"Wondering what Guy will say when he finds out about Celina and Reggie, and what will happen at the surprise party for Aunt Flora and Uncle Sven when you and Guy and Mattie Silverstone all show up."

"Mattie Silverstone?" Violet tried to place the name while unfastening her corset.

"She's Guy's neighbor. You met her the night you left for Boston. She rode into town on her piebald horse. Remember?"

Violet thought back while unlacing her shoes. The image of the piebald horse and the very stylish woman on it came to mind for the first time in a long, long while.

Rose continued. "She was quite friendly with Guy up until he left for the woods in October a year ago, and again this past summer until he left for the woods again. Some folks even wagered she'd get him to the altar before now."

"Is that so?" Violet replied thoughtfully. "Why hasn't anyone mentioned this to me in their letters?"

Rose yawned. "Grandma and Mama made me promise

148

not to. They say all the claims about Guy and Mattie being more than neighborly are hurtful rumors. I just thought you should know before you hear them from someone else."

"Thanks for telling me, Rose. Now hush. It's time to sleep." She pulled on her nightgown, removed the pins from her hair, turned out the lamp, and climbed into bed, wondering about the meaning of all that her sister had said. Although sleep quickly claimed her, troubling images of Guy with Mattie Silverstone woke her more than once.

When Christmas morning arrived, she knew that she would have to ask Guy about his friendship with this other woman. She would speak to him in private when an opportunity arose. For now, she would do her best to ignore the suspicions that were already rising up to steal away her joy.

Chapter

16

Three days later
The morning of December 28, 1889

As Violet sat in the parlor hemming flour sacks into
dishtowels for her Aunt Flora's housewarming later that
afternoon, she couldn't believe how quickly time had flown
by. Christmas morning had gone smoother than expected
with Guy and Louis concerning Celina's news of her marriage. After the initial surprise had worn off, her brothers
had each offered Reggie a hearty handshake and a pat on the
back. They had even joked about how to tell the similar-
looking brothers apart since Louis had lost his Stetson a
while ago and was back to wearing his black beret.

If any doubts had remained about Reggie's acceptance,
they were wiped out on the day after Christmas, when all
the Legards invited their friends, including Violet, Dan, and
Rose, to a sledding and tobogganing party. Reggie proved
to be both experienced and humorous on his downhill runs,
performing daredevil feats of speed and then clownish
antics that buried him in the snow on more than one occasion. The fun ended with an evening bonfire and hot chocolate, and even though Violet had spent the entire day with
Guy, she had not found a minute alone with him when she

could inquire about Mattie Silverstone.

Yesterday had proven equally busy, although Guy had not been a part of it. In the morning, she and Rose had helped her mother and grandmother with preparations for the surprise party tonight. In the afternoon Flora and Sven had brought all four of their children over to stay while they went up to Garden for supplies, and to take two lost dogs to a farmer who had advertised for their return. Time had passed quickly with Ola, Kal, Hope, and Daisy, ages eight, six, four, and one year. Violet wondered how Flora managed her brood, and the stray dogs and cats that she frequently rescued and placed in new homes. Working for the Connelly family and caring for only two small children seemed like a vacation by comparison.

She folded the third towel she had hemmed and picked up the fourth and last flour sack, thinking ahead to the afternoon here with Sven, Flora, and their children, and the big surprise they would encounter when they returned home for supper. So many plans had been put into place to keep the event a secret. Neighbors and friends would congregate at Richbourgs' down the road. They would then be shuttled to Sven and Flora's so no extra wagons or carriages would be visible at the Jorgensens' to tip them off on their return. Ladies would prepare the house, hanging new curtains, setting out new linens, arranging tables and chairs, and tending to food for the potluck dinner, while men would be furnishing the barn with equipment, supplies, and even some livestock. Violet wondered if the farmers had figured a way to keep the animals quiet until the surprise was revealed.

The question fled as quickly as it had come when she heard the voices of her mother, grandmother, and Rose at work in the kitchen, singing "Deck the Halls" in three-part harmony. Quietly, she sang along with them. Her needle moved swiftly through the fabric, her hemming and the song coming to completion at nearly the same moment. Violet was tying off her thread when she heard someone coming through the front door, and then the familiar but completely unexpected voice of Sven calling out.

"Mary? Lavinia? Anybody home?"

Violet hurried to greet him, getting there just ahead of the three from the kitchen. "Sven! We weren't expecting you until after lunch."

He pulled his brown plush hat from his head, his expression glum. "Sorry. Ola is sick. Flora sent me to pick up some medicine and to tell you we can't come."

Grandma said, "He seemed perfectly well yesterday. What's the matter?"

Sven shrugged. "Stuffy nose, coughing, a slight fever."

Lavinia said, "Sounds like a cold or a mild case of the flu."

Violet said, "No reason for the rest of you not to come. I'll go home with you and stay with him while you and Flora and the other children come here. I've had plenty of experience with sick children at the Connelly's. I'm sure Ola will be fine."

Sven remained thoughtful while Blackie circled him and then rubbed her face against his leg.

Rose said, "You've *got* to come, Uncle Sven! Your tenth anniversary only comes around once. We've all gone to a lot of trouble to help you celebrate, and we'll be mighty disappointed if you can't be here."

Sven shrugged and turned to Violet. "Dress warm. I'll take you home with me. But it will be up to Flora to decide."

Violet immediately pulled on her woolen cape, scarf, mittens and boots. Riding behind Sven on his horse proved both chilling and bumpy, but his surefooted gelding made his way steady and sure through snow and slush to the little farmhouse that Sven had completed a short while ago.

The arrival of Violet and the medicine, as well as a slight improvement in Ola, were enough to convince Flora to pack up the other children and head to town with Sven after their noonday meal. While Ola lay bedded down on the sofa near the warm parlor stove, Violet cleaned up the last of the dirty dishes, and set a pot of chicken broth on the stove to warm. Then she went to the parlor and checked on Ola.

He lay asleep, his breathing slightly impaired by some congestion in his nose. Checking his forehead with her hand, Violet could tell that he was a bit warmer than normal, but certainly not running a high fever. She prayed that he would soon return to good health. She was about to sit in the chair beside him when movement outside the window behind the sofa caught her attention.

A wagon carrying three people on the seat and a load of split wood in back rolled into the driveway and up to the barn. She knew by the black berets that these were Legards. While one of the men and the woman disappeared through the small side door into the barn, the other Legard started carrying wood to the shed at the side of the barn.

Violet sat down, pulled a lap robe over her, and put her feet on a stool near the stove. Through the window, she could see that gray skies had given way to sunshine, sending bright light into the parlor and offering the promise of good traveling weather tonight. She was praying that such would be the case when Ola awoke and spoke to her.

"Cousin Violet? May I please have some hot chocolate?"

Violet checked his forehead again and realized his fever

153

was gone. "Are you sure you want hot chocolate? I have some chicken broth ready."

Ola shook his head. "I want hot chocolate."

"How does your stomach feel?"

"Hungry!" he replied with a smile.

"Hot chocolate it is, then!" In the kitchen, Violet found cocoa powder in the cupboard and sugar in the canister, but the icebox held no milk. Even though milking time was three hours away, she was sure she could convince the family cow to produce enough for hot chocolate. With an explanation to Ola, she pulled on her cloak and boots, grabbed one of the empty pails by the back door, and headed toward the barn. One of the Legard men was still unloading wood, and when he greeted her she saw that it was Louis.

"Violet! What a surprise! I didn't know anyone was here."

"Ola wasn't feeling well, so I came to stay with him while the others went to town. Now, he's better and wants some hot chocolate, but there's no milk in the house, so I'm on my way to visit the cow."

"Guy's inside. He'll get some milk for you."

She nodded and went around to the side door. A beam of sunshine streamed through a nearby window lighting a scene that took her breath away. There stood Guy in very close proximity to the woman in the beret who had gotten off the wagon. She was *not* a Legard, however, but Mattie Silverstone! Guy was holding her face tenderly in both of his hands, gazing intently into her dark eyes, brushing a tear from her cheek and bending ever closer. In another second, their lips would meet.

"Excuse me!" Violet boldly interrupted.

Instantly Guy withdrew from Mattie and turned to her. "Violet! What are you doing here?"

"What are *you* doing here? Don't bother answering. I can see for myself! You're playing me the fool!" Her brown eyes sparked with anger. Then she turned on her heel and headed toward the stall occupied by the cow.

Guy followed her, determined to have his say. Catching her by the arm, he turned her toward him. "Violet, I can explain!"

"No explanation needed! Now, let go of me! I came to get milk for a sick child, then I'll be out of your way." She tried to free herself, but Guy's grip tightened.

"I'll get your milk after you hear me out. Mattie and I—"

The voice of Ola interrupted. "Cousin Violet? Did you get the milk?"

She looked back to find the eight-year-old just inside the door, coat pulled hastily over his pajamas, slippers covered with snow. Guy took the milk pail and released her. She hurried to the boy and picked him up. "You shouldn't be out here, Ola! You'll be sick all over again!"

"I'm hungry! I thought you'd need help milking Sidestep. She likes to kick the bucket."

"Mr. Legard will milk her. Now let's get inside!" She headed out the door.

Inside the house once more, she settled Ola beneath his blanket by the fire, placed his wet slippers on the hearth to dry, and offered to poach a couple of eggs to go with the hot chocolate he had requested.

When he eagerly accepted, she went to the kitchen to get to work, but she could not shake the vision of Guy preparing to kiss Mattie. The very thought of it made her seethe with jealousy. So upset was she, that she dropped one of the eggs before she could get it to the pan of water. She was in the process of cleaning up the floor when Guy came through the door with the milk.

"Violet, hear me out! There's nothing—"

She rose and spun around to face him, pulse racing. "Nothing! That's right! There's nothing you can say to explain what I saw with my own eyes! Now go, before I get so angry, I scream! And take this with you!" She pulled off the necklace he had given her and threw it at him.

He caught the necklace with his free hand, set down the milk pail, and left.

The moment the door closed, Violet began shaking uncontrollably, sobbing in silence. The sword of betrayal pierced her heart, and the pain was unbearable. But this was no time for tears. She had Ola to think of. Taking a deep breath, she dried her cheeks, rinsed out the egg-soaked rag, and turned her efforts to the jobs at hand. Through the back window, she could see that others were already arriving to make the house and barn ready for the surprise party. She must put all her energy into caring for Ola and helping where possible to make this celebration the best ever for Aunt Flora and Uncle Sven. She prayed she would some-how manage to disguise her sadness beneath the mask of congeniality on a night that would surely prove to be long and painful.

Chapter

17

Violet managed to put on a smile, a task made easier when she saw a classmate from her Sac Bay years coming through the back door carrying a pie basket.

"Hannah! How are you? We haven't seen each other since—I don't know when!"

"Good to see you, Violet!" She set her pie basket on the table and began unwrapping her cloak to reveal a generous figure even more plump than Violet remembered.

Buck Turkle followed Hannah through the door. He carried a bulging flour sack under his thick arm. "Violet Harrigan! Last time we met was … at that barn dance two years ago."

A scene of tumbling corn shocks and Guy coming to her rescue flashed in her mind.

Buck went on. "Did you hear? A year ago I made Hannah a Turkle, and now we have a little Turkle on the way!"

"I seem to remember my sister writing to me that you were wed. Congratulations! I'm so happy for you!"

He set the flour sack on the floor and gave Hannah a peck on the cheek. "See you later, Lovey."

Hannah's normally pink cheeks turned even redder.

The moment Buck departed, others streamed through the door with food and gifts—Sadie Schutt and Hannah's sister, Harriet Henry; Mattie's mother, Alvina Silverstone; Guy's mother Emelie and his sisters Lucy, Agnes, and Celina; and Mrs. Richbourg, among others. Violet moved quickly to prepare the hot chocolate and eggs, explaining about Ola while she worked.

Soon, the little fellow pushed his way through the crowd asking why all these people were in his mother's kitchen.

Violet explained. "These nice ladies have come to prepare a surprise party for your mama and papa for their tenth anniversary, and to help furnish your new house and barn with things they need to start farming. Now, go back to the sofa in the parlor and rest. I'll bring a tray with your hot chocolate and some poached eggs. All right?"

He pointed to a platter of ham slices that Mrs. Richbourg had set on the kitchen table. "May I please have some ham with my eggs?"

Mrs. Richbourg smiled. "Certainly! A growing boy needs meat! Now let's go and do as Violet says, and she'll bring you the ham and eggs." The plump woman took the small boy by the hand and led him away.

When Violet had served Ola, she returned to the kitchen to assist the other women, dreading the moment that Mattie would walk through the door to join them. An hour later, Violet went upstairs to hang new curtains in Ola and Kal's bedroom. Looking down at the farmyard below, she discovered the reason for Mattie's absence. The woman had evidently gone back home, and was returning now riding her piebald mare. Behind them on a lead trotted a stunning piebald colt. A moment later, half a dozen men, including Guy and his brothers and father, gathered around to admire the horseflesh, and then Mattie proudly led the colt into the barn. This animal was, evidently, Mattie's gift to Sven and Flora.

Anger and jealousy reared within Violet. The raven-haired beauty had stolen Guy's heart, and now it was obvious that she had gained the admiration of all the men on the premises. Violet's gift of flour sack towels seemed shamefully insignificant by comparison. She wanted to sit down and cry!

But this was no time for self-pity. There was much yet to do before her aunt and uncle returned. She headed downstairs to the large bedroom off the kitchen and searched in the trunk at the foot of the bed for the wedding costumes her aunt and uncle had worn ten years ago. When she found them, she carefully laid them out on the bed, and then she went to the parlor to help with the hanging of crepe streamers Mrs. Richbourg had brought for decorations. Afterward, she helped the ladies arrange the extra tables and chairs carried in by the men. By late afternoon, all the food, gifts, and decorations had been tended to, and word came from the men that the barn was also stocked and ready. Only one extra wagon stood on the property, and that had been hidden behind the barn so as not to be visible from the direction of Sven and Flora's approach. At a little past four, Joseph Legard, who had been posted at the end of the driveway to watch for Sven and Flora's return, announced that they were in sight. The family dogs, Rocky and Jack, began to bark and ran down the road to escort their loved ones home.

Men from the barn poured into the house, Mattie and Guy among them, but the couple who had been nose to nose in the barn now paid no attention to each other. The kitchen was jammed from wall to wall with people, while the table in the center stood equally crowded with food. A hush fell over the room. The excited barking of dogs and the voices of Flora and Sven and their three youngest could be heard as they approached the back stoop. Then came the sound of feet stamping snow off of boots.

The back door opened.

Flora entered first, carrying one-year-old Daisy in her arms.

Everyone shouted in unison.

"Surprise!"

Flora gasped. Daisy began to cry and her four-year-old sister, Hope, joined her.

Six-year-old Kal clung to his mother's skirt.

Sven's expression remained locked in a look of disbelief while neighbors and friends offered their anniversary greetings and well wishes on his new home and farm.

Mr. Richbourg explained the dual purpose of the celebration, concluding with, "Come out to the barn. There's plenty more surprises waiting."

Violet made sure Ola remembered to put on his coat, boots, and hat before she allowed him to go out the door. A carriage was just pulling into the driveway with William Burley at the reigns. A moment later, Violet's mother, sister, brother, and grandparents emerged and followed the others into the barn.

Alone in the house, Violet's curiosity about the farm furnishings overpowered her determination to avoid Guy and Mattie. Quickly she donned her cloak and headed for the barn, slipping inside to stand at the back while Sven and Flora and their children proceeded on a tour of discovery led by the tall and hefty Mr. Richbourg.

"This here's my old plow fixed up for you by Dan and Joseph. Mr. Burley, here, refurbished a run-down cultivator of Mr. Mercier's. That stack of leaky buckets came from Angus McAdams, 'ceptin' they don't leak no more, right Angus?"

"Guaranteed to hold water, or whatever else you need

160

them for!"

Mr. Richbourg continued. "Buck Turkle brought this here trough. Mr. Mercier gave ya these mangers. And the Legard gentlemen hauled a load of seasoned wood that's stacked out in your shed."

After words of heartfelt thanks by Sven and Flora, who were nearly too choked up to speak, Mr. Richbourg called attention to one more gift. Opening a stall, he led out the piebald colt and grinned. "I saved the best till last. I suppose ya can guess who gave ya this pretty little colt without me telling ya."

Sven nodded. "Miss Silverstone."

She stepped from the crowd with a radiant smile. "He's from good stock, a champion bloodline. He'll make a great rider for your boys once he's full-grown and trained. Or you can hitch him to a lightweight carriage or wagon. If need be, you can sell him at auction for a pretty penny and buy a draft horse. In any case, he's all yours!"

While Sven and Flora were offering their thanks, Guy was making his way out of the crowd, his gaze on Violet. She turned and headed for the house as fast as her feet could carry her. Hoping to set the record straight, Guy took off after Violet. Halfway to the house, he caught her firmly by the elbow and turned her to face him.

"Stop running from me, Violet and listen! What you saw between Mattie and me—"

His demands and piercing blue-eyed gaze could not check Violet's reply that flowed fast in an angry stream. "I know what I saw! I surely don't need you to explain it! I've been your fool, but no more!" Yanking free, she lifted her skirt and sped toward the stoop, but not fast enough to escape Guy's words.

"You *are* a fool, Violet! For not listening!"

161

She closed the door behind her and flung off her cape, tossing it onto a peg and darting into the master bedroom to gain control of her emotions. In mere moments the house would be filled with guests and Flora and Sven would be compelled to come into this room to change into their wedding costumes. Violet gazed at the bridal dress and suit and wondered how her aunt and uncle had managed to stay happily married for ten years, when she herself could not even surmount the obstacles of courtship. Dabbing at the tears that threatened to spill down her cheeks, she took a deep breath, swallowed past the lump in her throat, and put on a smile before returning to the kitchen that was fast filling with hungry guests.

Lacking an appetite, she waited until the rest had passed through the buffet line before taking a plate in hand and adding a slice of ham, a spoonful of baked beans, and a sweet roll. She found a seat near Harriet and Hannah and caught up on their news, then told of her own life since moving to Boston. From the corner of her eye, she watched Guy and Mattie. They were seated on opposite sides of the room from one another and never once exchanged glances. Instead, Guy engaged in conversation with Mr. Richbourg and Mr. Mercier while Mattie sat between Guy's brother Louis, and his sister, Agnes. Violet was further puzzled by the fond glances passing between Mattie and Louis. One time, their heads bent close to one another for some secret exchange and then they both glanced across the room at Violet. Embarrassed to be caught staring at them, Violet turned away and then offered to replenish Hannah's and Harriet's plates, thankful for a reason to leave the room.

After the guests had eaten their fill of the buffet, Mrs. Richbourg led the anniversary couple on a tour of the gifts that had been brought to furnish the house, including the bedroom curtains, sofa cover, and kitchen linens. Violet cringed at the paltriness of her modest contribution, but her aunt spoke as appreciatively of the flour sack towels as she did of the larger items.

When they returned to the parlor, Violet's grandfather initiated a round of reminiscences about the honored couple starting with the story of their first quarrelsome encounter outside the Machine Shop at Fayette. Each guest offered a memory of touching or humorous quality, often concerning the many cats and dogs Flora had rescued and given away, until the story of the Jorgensens' married life had been told. Then, the men pushed the parlor furniture back to the walls and rolled up the rugs. Mr. Richbourg took up his fiddle and Mr. Burley pulled a mouth organ from his pocket, playing bright harmonic tones that started feet tapping. Flora and Sven danced the first dance, a waltz, and then a variety of musical rhythms from polkas to two-steps to good old-fashioned contra-dances brought their company, a few couples at a time, to the small dance floor.

Violet danced a polka with her brother, a two-step with her grandfather, and a gallop with Buck Turkle who, to her amazement proved to be a terpsichorean wonder. While the music continued, Violet helped Rose put Ola, Kal, and Hope to bed upstairs. Little Daisy had fallen asleep earlier and lay peacefully in her crib in the master bedroom, seemingly unaware of the party that had been gradually increasing in volume.

With the children down for the night, Violet and her sister retreated to the kitchen where their grandmother along with Mrs. Richbourg and Mrs. Mercier were putting away food and washing dishes. The gay tunes from the parlor drifted in, playing counterpart to the choleric emotions Violet held within. She longed for the evening to end so that she could retreat to her own private place of pain. How she wished that she were leaving for Boston on the morrow. But that was impossible.

After Violet and the others had been in the kitchen for awhile, the Legard women came to spell them, insisting that they return to the party. When Violet balked, Celina guided her to the parlor, allowing no room for argument. Violet retreated to a corner of the room where she wished she could shrink to the size of a mouse and scurry away unseen.

Instead, Reggie sought her out, ignoring her polite refusal to dance and insisting that she partner with him on a polka. When the music ended, he fixed her with a steady gaze and spoke quietly but firmly.

"I know what happened. You're wrong about Guy. You'll see." With no further explanation, he ushered her back to the corner where he had found her.

Violet dismissed Reggie's cryptic statement, spoken with the unfailing confidence that had sometimes proven his downfall. Through jigs and reels she smiled and clapped her hands, but inside her heart was breaking and she longed for the evening to come to an end.

Finally, at half-past midnight, Mr. Richbourg said, "Folks, there'll be one last dance, a waltz. But before I play, two happy couples have announcements to make. First, Widow Harrigan and Mr. Burley."

William ushered Violet's mother to the center of the parlor where her beaming smile lit every corner of the room before she began to speak. "Mr. Burley and I cordially invite you all to our wedding reception, also known as a New Year's Eve party, to take place at the Music Hall beginning at nine o'clock on the thirty-first of this month. Please come and help us celebrate!"

Cheers and congratulations filled the air, dying out only

after Mr. Richbourg raised his hands in a gesture for silence. "Thank you, Widow Harrigan, and best wishes on your upcoming nuptials! Now, Mr. Louis Legard and Miss Mattie Silverstone have somethin' to say."

They came from opposite sides of the room, joining hands when they met. Their faces glowed with happiness as they briefly gazed into one another's eyes, then turned to take in those assembled. Louis began to speak.

"Folks, there's been a lot of conjecture about this young lady over the last year or more. Some of you even made bets she would get my brother Guy to the altar by now. You thought he was paying calls on her. Not so. *I* was the one. You mistook me for my brother when I lost my Stetson and went back to wearing my beret."

Mattie began to speak. "The fact is, Guy Legard has never stepped foot inside my folks' place. Isn't that right, Mama and Daddy?"

Her parents confirmed her statement.

Louis continued. "Then this afternoon, when Guy and Mattie were in the barn preparing a place for her colt, a piece of straw got into her eye. It hurt so much, Guy took her over to the window to get a close look. Right then, in came someone else—I won't say who—and saw them standing nose to nose. Then that other person ran off all wrongheaded and was convinced that Guy was sweet on Mattie." He paused to look directly at Violet, his gaze remaining on her while he continued. "The fact is, Mattie and I were planning to announce our betrothal after I come back from the woods in April, but to set the record straight, we decided to announce it right now!"

Mattie quickly added, "A June wedding is planned and you are all invited!"

Chapter

18

Cheers and whistles went up. Folks gathered around Mattie and Louis, offering their congratulations.

Violet could hardly believe her ears. It had been Louis instead of Guy that had caused all the rumors, and a piece of straw that had brought Guy so close to Mattie that it looked like they were going to kiss. How Violet regretted not listening when Guy had tried to explain! What a big fool she had been! Overwhelmed with relief and remorse, she looked for Guy, desperate to offer an apology. A moment later, she felt a tap on the shoulder. When she turned around, Guy pulled her close.

In his strong embrace, she broke into tears. "I … I'm so sorry! Can you … ever forgive me?"

"Hush, *ma petite amie. Je t'aime!*" He offered her his handkerchief and gently cradled her in his arms.

Mr. Richbourg began to play the last waltz, and they moved across the floor as one. When the music ended, Guy took the violet pendant from his pocket and placed it around her neck. Violet's heart flooded with joy and love, and she wished that she never had to part from Guy again.

Too soon, reality set in. Guests were searching for coats, boots, and hats, and departing to climb onto the two wagons available to haul folks to the Richbourgs', where their own rigs were waiting. Guy pulled Violet near.

"I must go. I'll see you soon. *Bonsoir, ma petite amie.*" He kissed her on the forehead and then, with a reluctance that tore at his heart, he headed out the door.

Within minutes Violet, too, departed to climb into the carriage that had brought her family. A cold wind blew from the north, sending snow into swirls and threatening to chill her to the bone. But the warmth in her heart remained, bringing comfort and peace and constant thoughts of Guy.

The next afternoon, when the Sunday dinner dishes had been cleaned up, Violet, Rose, Grandma, and Blackie, joined Lavinia, Dan, Grandpa, and William in the parlor where preparations for the wedding and New Year's Eve party at the Town Hall were under discussion.

Grandpa described the best location for gathering greens. "There's a stand of cedars north of here by about three miles. The company owns it and won't mind a bit if we gather—" Loud taps of the doorknocker interrupted his words. "I'll get it."

Violet prayed that Guy had come to call. A moment later, Grandpa returned to the parlor, a grin lighting his face. "Violet, Rose, Dan, please come to the entryway. Some charming gentlemen have an invitation they would like to extend."

The three quickly obeyed, finding Guy and Joseph bundled warmly in their heaviest winter jackets, scarves, and berets. Guy spoke first.

"Would you like to join us on a sleigh ride?"

Joseph explained. "We're going up to Guy's house. Celina, Reggie, Louis, and Mattie are already there warming the place up and making some hot chocolate for us."

Violet's heart leaped with joy. Seeing eagerness in the eyes of her siblings, she said, "We'd love to go!"

Grandpa said, "Dress warm, now. I'll get some blankets."

Guy said, "No need, Mr. McAdams. We have blankets, fur robes, and foot warmers."

He smiled. "Then there's nothing left but for you young folks to have a nice time. I'll tell the others." He started for the parlor.

Dan stopped him with a question. "Grandpa, what about the greens for the Town Hall?"

"Don't give it another thought, Son. William and I will take care of it."

Within minutes, Violet, Dan, and Rose were ensconced in Hudson Bay blankets and buffalo robes and their feet were nestled on foot warmers. Once underway, Violet pulled her scarf up over her mouth and nose, and tugged her stocking cap down over her ears and forehead until only her eyes were exposed.

Two huge draft horses made light work of the sleigh, trotting easily through the fallen snow to carry their passengers at a comfortable pace out of town and along the country road. After a short while, Guy slowed the horses to a walk, and fifteen minutes later he pulled to a halt outside a charming little frame house made of cedar siding. A veranda stretched across the entire width of the place, protecting the front door and window. On the left end stood a small chimney that sent the welcomed essence of wood smoke into the cold air. Behind the house stood an outhouse, and beyond it, a small barn painted iron oxide red.

Guy and Joseph helped Violet and Rose down from the sleigh and then Guy drove the rig into the barn. While he tended to the team, Violet went inside with Joseph, Dan, and Rose.

Celina greeted them, adding their coats to empty pegs that lined a wall of the one-room house. A cot and stool had been pulled up near the single-burner potbelly stove where Mattie stood stirring a large pan of cocoa. On the wall to her right hung two shelves that served as cupboards. A small table nearby held mugs waiting to be filled. Beyond it, a window curtained in muslin looked out onto a cleared field, and beneath it stood a dry sink.

Celina said, "What do you think of Guy's place, Violet? Spare, isn't it?"

Violet smiled. "I'd call it cozy. Who made the curtains?" Her gaze strayed to Mattie who shook her head.

Celina said, "Agnes made them."

Joseph said, "I helped Guy build the table, chair, dry sink and cot, and hang the shelves."

Louis said, "And I helped him install the stove."

Reggie, who stood warming his hands by the stove, offered a winning smile. "And I thank you all for making this gathering warm in temperature, temperament, and taste."

Mattie's dark brows narrowed. "You're a little ahead of yourself. We haven't gotten to the taste part yet."

Reggie laughed. "I believe in the power of positive prophecies. I have every confidence that we are about to experience the 'taste' aspect."

Ladling a small amount of cocoa into a mug, Mattie sipped it and smiled. "Time to pour the cocoa."

While the mugs were being filled, Guy came inside, hung his coat and beret on a peg, and joined Violet, slipping his arm about her waist. "What do you think of my place, *ma petite amie?*"

Violet gazed up into his questioning blue eyes and smiled. "I'd say it's just right. You have everything you need and not one thing more—except for all these extra mugs once we're done with our cocoa."

Mattie laughed. "These are *borrowed* mugs. They go back to my mama's kitchen when we're through. You never know who might come to call when the holidays arrive." She gazed fondly at Louis. Then, setting aside the near-empty pan, she said, "Drink up, everyone!"

Guy said, "Wait! I propose a toast. To Louis and Mattie—may they enjoy a carefree betrothal and, come spring, a blessed union!"

"Cheers!" echoed amongst the company and then the ladies settled on the cot and chair, while the fellows took seats on the floor. Conversation ranged from the wedding of Reggie and Celina, to the upcoming nuptials of Violet's mother and Mr. Burley, to the yet unplanned wedding of Louis and Mattie.

Violet glanced often at Guy. He smiled when he caught her looking at him. Other times, unaware of her gaze, he appeared almost melancholy. She wondered if he was dreading their upcoming separation as much as she was. Putting reality aside, she imagined for a moment what it might be like if he didn't go back to lumber camp, and she didn't return to Boston. This cabin would indeed be a snug, though spare little haven and for a moment she could see herself cooking a pot of stew for their dinner at the one-burner stove. Then, Celina posed a question to Rose that stood as a stark reminder of the lean times that had come to the area.

"How do you fill your days, now that your mama's boardinghouse is closed?"

Pressing a wavy red tress back from her face, she read-ily answered. "I help with the chores at Grandma's. I wash the dishes after every meal, and sometimes I do the cook-ing. I'm really good at stew. I can make it out of just about anything—venison, rabbit, squirrel, whitefish—whatever

170

Grandpa brings home. Other times I dust furniture and beat carpets. When chores are done, I used to go and visit my friends, but there's hardly anyone my age left in town. Now, I fill my extra time sitting by the parlor stove and reading, or working on embroidery." She pulled out a hand-kerchief with a particularly lovely rosebud embroidered in the corner.

Celina studied the piece and smiled. "Very nice work, Rose." Her gaze shifted to look straight into the younger girl's brown eyes. "Have you ever considered moving away from Fayette? Reggie and I would love to have you come and live with us in Boston. You would be our maid and cook, tending to the same things you're doing at your grandma's. For me, it would be almost like having a younger sister, except you'd get paid!"

Reggie said, "You'd be near Violet, and I know she'll come visit us often now that we have a place of our own. Right, Violet?"

Violet nodded. Seeing a doubtful look on her sister's face, she told Reggie, "You'll have to promise to give Rose the same day off that I have so I can show her the city—*if* she wants to go to Boston, that is. What do you think, Rose?"

She shrugged and offered a tentative smile. "I don't know. Do you suppose Mama would allow me to go?"

Reggie said, "I'm sure she would. Knowing that you would be working for friends and living near Violet—she's got to say 'yes.' Besides, there's not much of a future for you in Fayette."

Rose said, "If I come live with you, would I be able to go to school again? I dream of getting a high school diploma."

Reggie and Celina exchanged glances, then Reggie

replied. "If school is what you want, then to school you will go. But you will be attending classes at night with other folks who work during the day."

Rose nodded thoughtfully.

Celina said, "You think it over. No need to decide today."

Conversation moved on, the fellows drifting to talk of farming, fishing, and shipbuilding while the ladies spoke of friends, family, and faith. After a few minutes, Guy rose and drew Violet away from the others.

"Come outside. I want to show you the barn."

Violet detected a gleam of pride in his blue eyes and readily agreed.

When they started to put on their coats, Louis asked, "Is the party over already?"

Guy shook his head. "I'm going to show Violet the barn."

Reggie chortled. "And steal a kiss, I'll wager!"

Violet wagged her finger. "Not so! Any kisses exchanged will be given freely!"

Louis said, "Don't be so sure. *Frère Guy* has hung mistletoe from the rafters!"

Violet turned to Guy in surprise.

He shook his head. "Louis fibs. Come, and I will show you." To the others, he said, "We'll only be a few minutes."

Joseph said, "No hurry. We won't leave without you!"

On her way out the door, Violet overheard Reggie saying to Joseph, "Maybe you ought to show Rose the barn," followed by her sister's adamant refusal and her brother's hearty laugh.

Violet was still smiling at the humorous exchanges when Guy's arm wrapped tightly about her waist and guided her toward the barn.

He gazed down at the young woman by his side who was smiling from her brown eyes to the tip of her chin. "Having a good time, *ma petite amie?*"

Violet nodded, her head still swimming with the possibility of Rose moving to Boston. Those thoughts fled when she entered the barn and Guy pointed upward.

"See? No mistletoe. That Louis is a real jokester." He turned her toward him, tilting her face upward with a finger beneath her chin.

She could see the love in his blue-gray eyes, and it stirred a longing within to feel his lips against hers.

Guy could barely contain the passion within for the budding young girl who had opened into a beautiful blossom before his very eyes. He struggled to keep his desire under control, bending close to press a brief kiss to her waiting lips.

"*Je t'aime, ma petite amie.*"

These words, though little more than a whisper, revealed unmistakable passion. And then he continued.

"How I wish we could stay here, the two of us, and make a life together. But there is still much to do. Next summer, I will have enough money to drill a well and buy farm equipment. A year after that, I will buy a larger stove for the house, and some livestock for the barn. Then, I will not need to go to lumber camp anymore. Promise me, *ma petite amie,* that you will come home from Boston then, and marry me."

"I promise!" Violet replied.

Guy wrapped his arms tightly about her, lifted her off her feet, and swung her around. When she touched the ground again, he took her face in his hands and gazed into her eyes. Then his lips descended to hers so gently she barely felt the brush of his soft mustache.

Too soon, the kiss ended. After a moment's contemplation, he said, "Our promise is sealed with a kiss. But our wedding day is so far off, it is best not to speak of our betrothal for a while."

Violet nodded.

Guy slipped his arm about her and walked her toward the house. To Violet, it seemed as if she was floating on a cloud of love, until she stepped inside the house and heard Reggie and Celina speaking of life in Boston. Suddenly, the remaining days in Fayette seemed far too short and the next year-and-a-half in Boston seemed far too long. But what could she do to change it?

Chapter

19

Behind a dressing screen near the parlor stove in the Maple Room, Violet sank into a tub of warm water to bathe for her mother's wedding and New Year's Eve reception. While working up a mound of suds, her gaze rose to the border of maple leaves that had been stenciled just below the ceiling. Though a bit faded, it held wonderful charm and memories of her great-grandmother, and blended perfectly with the other decor that made the room inviting. The maple leaf quilt and matching pillow on the bed, the hand-hooked rug with a large maple leaf in its center, the wardrobe with carved maple leaves on its doors, the black chair with brilliant gold maple leaves painted on its back. All of these reminded Violet of her Canadian heritage and the loving old woman who had lived here.

Violet's thoughts now turned to more immediate concerns, sending her mood swinging on a pendulum between happiness and dread. Although thrilled for her mother and the life she was about to begin with William Burley, Violet could barely stand to think of how fast time was passing, and how quickly Guy would be returning to lumber camp. She sighed. There was nothing she could do to slow the clock, but she *could* choose to look on the bright side. This evening would be a wonderful celebration of new beginnings, and she intended to enjoy every moment.

A few days from now, when she returned to Boston,

Rose would go with her. How thrilled she was that her younger sister would be living nearby, and that she would be working for friends and able to take advantage of educational and cultural opportunities not available at Fayette, even in the best of times.

As for life at the Connellys, Violet had much to look forward to. First, there were the children, Patrick and Katherine, delightful in temperament and a pleasure to care for. She would enjoy watching them grow over the next eighteen months. In addition, Mrs. Connelly had promised her short trips to New York and Philadelphia and a much longer journey to the British Isles and the continent in the upcoming months. If Violet could not spend the next year-and-a-half with Guy, at least she could welcome the opportunity for travel. Her thoughts drifted to the sea and the ocean voyage in her future, scenes of quaint Irish cottages and narrow country lanes filling her mind according to the descriptions Mrs. Connelly had given.

A knock on the door and the voice of her mother brought her back to Fayette and the present.

"Violet, are you almost done? Your grandmother and I need to prepare ourselves for the wedding now."

"One minute, Mama!"

Stepping from the tub, she quickly dried herself, shooed Blackie off her robe, then pulled it on and headed upstairs to fix her hair and put on the velvet gown she had worn at Celina's wedding.

When Violet and her family climbed the stairs to the Music Hall two hours later, she could hear the musicians warming up, and when she entered the room, she smiled at the way its appearance had changed from utilitarian to festive. Greens tied with large white bows and decorated with

176

silver bells adorned the walls and stage. Against the right wall stood a table adorned with more greens and bows, and laden with a punch bowl, a four-tiered cake, and a generous assortment of cookies, crackers, sausage, and cheese. Nearby, chairs lined both sides of a long table that held centerpieces of greens, white bows, and silver bells. There, guests could enjoy the tasty refreshments while the left side of the room's polished maple floor accommodated the dancing.

With all in readiness, the wedding party took their places and the marriage ceremony began. At arm's length from Violet stood her mother, radiant and beautiful in the blue satin gown she had sewn and seeded with tiny pearls. Beside her, William was hardly recognizable with his normally shaggy hair, beard, and mustache razor trimmed, and his charcoal gray suit tailored to smoothly cover his round girth. The vows were quietly exchanged and then the closing words of the solemn, yet joyful ceremony brought an ever-increasing smile to the groom's countenance.

"Forasmuch as Lavinia and William have consented together in holy wedlock, and have witnessed the same before God and this company, and thereto have pledged their faith either to other, and have declared the same by joining of hands; I pronounce that they are husband and wife together, in the name of the Father, and of the Son, and of the Holy Ghost. Those whom God hath joined together, let no man put asunder. Amen…You may kiss the bride."

With gentleness belying the groom's size and teamster occupation, he pressed his lips briefly to his bride's. The moment the kiss ended, Chase and his musician friends struck up *Gary Owen*, the first tune Lavinia and Mr. Burley had danced to the summer before last. Without hesitation, the newlyweds headed for the center of the dance floor. A

177

couple of minutes later, they insisted that the rest of the family join them.

Violet and her sister and brother formed a trio of dancers, like they had when their father had been alive and played the very same tune on his whistle. While heel- toe- ing to the rhythm of the tune, Violet sensed her father's spirit in the joyfulness, and imagined him smiling as he looked down from heaven.

Before the jig ended, Guy and the rest of his family arrived, quickly cast aside their winter coats and black berets, and joined in the dance, giving it a new momentum that kept the musicians playing. A couple of minutes later, Violet saw her grandfather ushering her grandmother to a chair beside the refreshment table and offering her some punch. For a moment, Violet worried that the activity had been too much for the elderly woman, but her smile and wave put concerns aside, and Violet danced on. When the musicians finally fell silent, an out-of-breath groom led his bride to the refreshment table where Grandma was now on her feet and serving punch to all for a toast.

Grandpa smiled broadly and held his cup high. "To Mr. and Mrs. Burley. May the Lord bless you and keep you. May he make his face to shine upon you, in your going out and your coming in, in your rising up and your lying down, in your waking and your sleeping, until the day comes when there is no sunset and no dawning!"

"Cheers!" echoed through the crowd.

Violet's cup touched Guy's and he smiled, but in his blue eyes was a far-away look. She wondered, as she sipped, whether he was thinking the same thought as she— someday, the toast would be for them.

Within Guy burned a longing for the day when there would be no more good-byes, only togetherness with the redheaded, brown-eyed beauty who had held his heart captive from the time of her birth.

That notion vanished amidst the arrival and greetings of guests who had been at the party three nights ago. Violet's Aunt Flora, Uncle Sven, and their children entered, followed by the Silverstones, Turkles, Richbourgs and Merciers. In addition, several from the village entered the room—Dr. and Mrs. Sadler, Postmaster Rowe and his wife, Mr. and Mrs. McCumby who managed the hotel, the village blacksmith Mr. Cumberland and his wife, and the furnace founder Mr. Flynn and his wife—among others.

While the musicians played quietly, guests offered their congratulations to the newlyweds and then wandered over to the refreshment table. Violet helped her grandmother cut and serve the cake while Rose filled punch cups. When all had been served, Guy led Violet to the table where sat the McCumbys, Flynns, and Sadlers. Mr. McCumby greeted Guy cordially.

"Good to see you, again, Mr. Legard. I noticed your brother is here, too, but I didn't find your names on the hotel registry for this evening."

Guy shook his head. "We will go home to Sac Bay with the rest of my family when we've seen the New Year in."

No sooner had he spoken, than a gust of wind rattled the window behind him, pelting it with sleet and sending a chill up Violet's spine.

Mr. McCumby smiled. "As you wish. We have vacant rooms, if the weather should force a change of plans."

Guy acknowledged the offer with a nod.

Dr. Sadler said, "Sounds like 1890 could blow in on a storm from the north."

Mr. McCumby raised his punch cup. "Storm or no, here's to full rooms and hot furnaces in the year to come."

"To hot furnaces!" Said Mr. Flynn, clinking his cup against Mr. McCumby's.

All drank to the toast, and then pleasant conversation followed about the thickness of ice in the harbor, Violet's experiences in Boston, births and deaths attended by the doctor, and travelers served by the McCumbys. The discussion came to an end when the musicians struck up a two-step, bringing young and old alike to their feet. While Violet partnered with Sven, Guy took Flora around the room. At one end of the dance floor, Rose made sure that Ola, Kal, Hope, and Daisy joined in the fun of the lively tune, and then she bundled them up to take them to her grandparents' for the remainder of the evening.

With hours to go before midnight, one dance followed another in rapid succession, and so did Violet's partners. Guy, Buck, Louis, Grandpa, Mr. Burley, Mr. Legard, Mr. Richbourg, Mr. Silverstone, Mr. Mercier, Dan, Joseph, and Dr. Sadler who had succeeded Dr. Phillips as the Company doctor, took their turns. Then Mr. McCumby, who had evidently gone across the road to check on business at the hotel, came inside covered with snow. He made a beeline for Violet's mother, and after exchanging a few words and a nod with her, he stepped onto the stage where the musicians were playing. With a word to Chase, the waltz came to an end and a strong chord sounded, signaling the need for silence.

Mr. McCumby addressed the assembly. "While we've been partying, old Jack Frost has come to visit and piled up snow drifts so high that those of you who live outside the village will not get home tonight."

Buck Turkle sent a worried look in Hannah's direction. Mattie conferred with her folks in hushed tones, and Mr. Legard began gathering his family near.

McCumby continued. "Don't worry, folks. I have rooms for some of you at the hotel, and the rest of you can bed down at the boardinghouse that Mrs. Burley used to run."

Violet's mother took the stage. "Friends, it is now but a few minutes to midnight. No need to leave before we see the old year out. Chase will play a polka for us. At ten seconds before 12 o'clock, we'll count the New Year in, and then he'll play one last waltz. Find a partner!"

Grandpa slipped his arm around Violet while Guy led her grandmother, who had spent the evening serving punch, onto the floor. Around the room they went. Violet caught glimpses of her grandmother stepping to the tune, and thought that she had never looked livelier. Despite concerns about the weather, the guests happily counted the old year out and the New Year in. Then, as planned, Chase struck up the last waltz.

While Guy guided Violet around the floor, she tried not to think of how she would miss him when he returned to lumber camp. Instead, she looked ahead to the plans they had made for the future.

But the pleasant thought fled when, from the other end of the room rose the sound of folks gasping in fear followed by her grandfather's desperate plea.

"Dr. Sadler! Dr. Sadler! Come here!"

Chapter

20

Panic pierced Violet's heart. Desperate to get to the other end of the room, she pushed past couples who had stopped dancing. There on the floor lay her grandmother, while her grandfather knelt by her side.

"Mary! Wake up," he pleaded frantically, shaking her shoulders. But she remained motionless.

Violet dropped to her knees beside the beloved woman, pressing a hand to her cheek. "Grandma! Say something!"

The elderly woman made no response.

A moment later, Lavinia knelt down, taking her mother's hand in hers. "Mama! Mama, talk to me!"

Dr. Saddler approached, issuing orders.

"Stand back! Everybody stand back!"

Though reluctant to obey, Violet allowed Guy's strong arms to lift her to her feet and lead her away. Tears began to flow.

He ushered her to a chair, sat close beside her, and pulled out his handkerchief, tenderly drying her wet cheeks.

Violet took Guy's handkerchief and covered her face, sobbing quietly.

"Hush, *ma petite amie,* hush." He wrapped his arm tightly about her and cradled her head against his chest, praying silently for a miracle.

A few minutes later, her mother and Dan approached.

Violet gazed up at their tearstained cheeks and knew what her mother was about to say.

"Mama's gone." A sob caught in Lavinia's throat. She regained control and then added, "Dr. Saddler said she had a stroke."

Violet nodded, sorrow surging within.

Her mother sat beside her and they hugged while Dan stood near. After a short while, Grandpa joined them, struggling against his tears to speak.

"Some men … have gone to build a coffin…Their wives will prepare the body at Dr. Saddler's. We'll hold calling hours in the parlor tomorrow afternoon starting at two o'clock. I'll begin the funeral service at four. Let's go home now. There's nothing more we can do here."

With Guy's help, Violet managed to find her boots and cloak. He wrapped his arm tightly about her and together, they stepped out into the blizzard and trudged through knee-high drifts that had obscured the road home. There, her family gathered in the parlor. While William, Guy, Joseph, and Reggie sat quietly by, Celina made and served tea.

Blackie meowed pitifully as she roamed the house, presumably in search of Grandma.

In the wee morning hours, when Blackie had settled quietly in Violet's lap, she carried the cat up to bed. Rose came up soon after, whimpering quietly as she climbed beneath her covers. Fitful, nightmarish sleep filled the hours until mid-morning when Violet awoke. She could hear the voices of Ola, Kal, Hope, and Daisy, who had spent the night with their parents in the Maple Room on the first floor and were now ready to play.

Beneath the children's chatter ran the lower tones of Guy and her grandfather. Violet rose, washed, and dressed, descending to the first floor while her sister slept on.

Though bereft of an appetite, at the urging of Guy and others, Violet ate a small portion of bacon and eggs prepared by Celina.

A little later, when Rose had come down, Violet helped her mother and sister prepare the house for the arrival of the deceased, covering all the mirrors and draping the windows with black crepe as custom demanded. Guy, Dan, Joseph, and her grandfather rearranged parlor furniture to make room for the coffin. Extra chairs were brought from the Music Hall and then, with all in readiness, the men carried in the oak box. Soon, neighbors and friends arrived, expressing their condolences and offering to supply meals for the next few days. With Guy constantly by her side, Violet found the strength to keep her tears to a trickle. Many of the folks who had so cheerfully attended the New Year's Eve celebration now somberly arrived to express their condolences.

At four o'clock, Violet's family and the closest of friends, neighbors, and Company men remained in the parlor for the service. Guy held Violet near, praying for God's comforting hand to ease her loss. Her grandfather stood in front of the coffin, opened his Bible, and began to read from the Gospel of John.

"'I am the resurrection, and the life: he that believeth in me, though he were dead, yet shall he live: and whosoever liveth and believeth in me shall never die.'" He followed with additional passages from Job and the Psalms, ending with words from the First Epistle to the Corinthians. "'Therefore, my beloved brethren, be ye steadfast, unmovable, always abounding in the work of the Lord, forasmuch as ye know that your labor is not in vain in the Lord.'"

After a moment's pause, he closed the Good Book. Surveying the room with an all-encompassing glance of deeply saddened blue eyes, he began to eulogize. "Today we celebrate the life of Mary Ferguson McAdams. She is not here." He indicated the coffin. "She has ascended before us to claim her room in the heavenly mansion that has been prepared for her by her Lord and Savior, Jesus Christ. And while we grieve our loss, let us take solace in the promise of our Lord Jesus of life everlasting for those who believe in Him, as did Mary.

"Aside from her unwavering faith in Christ, Mary loved being a wife, mother, grandmother, and devoted daughter to the care of her own mother. In all of this, I know of no one who surpassed Mary McAdams. Whether raising her three children, tending her failing mother, or soothing a crying grandchild, she remained patient and gentle.

"In addition to her love of family, Mary held a special passion for the education of our town's children. When we first arrived in Fayette back in the fall of 1867, there was no school for the little ones, and so Mary began teaching right here in our dining room. Later, when the school had been built, she made a point to invite each teacher to tea and to offer words of encouragement as they sometimes struggled to meet the demands of their profession.

"In recent years, Mary devoted much of her time to the increasing number of grandchildren born into our family. Nothing made her happier than to be surrounded by these little ones and to watch them grow."

At that moment, Blackie meowed and then leaped from the floor to a nearby table and then to the coffin where she let out a mournful wail.

Angus took the crying feline under his arm, stroked her, and offered a sad smile. "I would be remiss in not mentioning the new comfort Mary found in Blackie during these last few years. Until she came on the scene, Mary never much cared for cats, but Blackie proved good company when Mary suffered her spells. While she recovered, Blackie would curl up in her lap or nestle beside her on the bed. And as you have just seen, Blackie would remain by Mary even now, giving testimony of her loyalty to her mistress. Now that Blackie and I have said our piece, I invite you to share your cherished memories of Mary."

Violet's mother rose to speak. "I'll never forget the day I introduced my mother to William. 'I hear you dance a lively jig,' she said. He started to hum *Durang's Hornpipe,* squatting down to heel-toe his way around her. She laughed and started to dance the jig, too. And so, without a word, William won Mama's heart and ever after they were on the best of terms. I'm so thankful she lived long enough to see us…" Tears choked off the rest of her words and she returned to her seat and the comfort of her new husband's embrace.

Violet stood up and faced the funeral guests. "I remember the first time I helped Grandma bake taffy tarts. She had come to stay with us in Sac Bay when Rose was born. We baked them again when Hope was born. I can't believe…" A lump began to form in her throat. "…I can't believe Grandma won't be here to bake tarts when the next baby is born." Tears spilled down her cheeks and she swiftly returned to her seat.

Flora spoke next. "I remember when Mama gave me my first dog, Stubby. I'd had a fox cub for a pet, but he'd been killed and I was devastated. Mama figured the best way to get me over my loss was to turn my attention to a new puppy. I've often thought that she might have done differently if she'd known how much I would come to love dogs, and how many of them I would bring home over the years." She offered a smile that quickly turned sad, sparking new tears.

Sven rose to speak, making one quiet statement that spoke volumes. "No man could ask for a better mother-in-law than Mary McAdams."

Big Toby, who worked at the hotel, and a few other townsfolk contributed their memories, and then the mourners took their leave and the men who had carried in the coffin removed it to a place of storage where it would remain until spring when a grave could be opened. Guy, Dan, Joseph, William, and Grandpa returned the extra chairs to the Music Hall and restored the furniture to the parlor while Violet helped Celina prepare tea to go with the cookies and cakes that had been brought by neighbors.

When everyone gathered in the parlor again, Violet settled next to Guy on the sofa. While Reggie regaled his listeners with a humorous story about a funeral he once attended in Boston—a story that Violet suspected was more fiction than fact—she couldn't help thinking about one more heartache that was yet to come on this day of sorrow. Tonight she must bid Guy farewell, for early tomorrow morning he and Louis would head north to find work at another lumber camp. She gazed up at the man who had watched over her from her infancy—the kind, compassionate man she had pledged to marry—and wondered how she could stand to be away from him for the next year-and-a-half. In his blue eyes, she read his wordless message of love and sadness.

Guy dreaded the thought of leaving Violet. A little while later, he offered his good-byes to the others, and she saw him to the door.

He pulled on his heavy coat, black beret, and scarf, and then pulled her close. *"Je t'aime, ma petite amie."*

She closed her eyes and he covered her mouth with his,

187

tasting the sweetness of her lips. He tightened his hold, pressing her firmly to him and drinking deeply of the nectar she offered.

Violet's heart raced. She never wanted this kiss to end. Then suddenly, he released her, pulled on his gloves, and with a quiet, *"Adieu,"* he headed out the door.

"Write to me, Guy!" she called after him.

He acknowledged her request with a wave of his hand, and then disappeared into the dark of night.

Chapter

21

June 21, 1890

Guy stood and raised his glass. "To the new Mr. and Mrs. Legard. May God bless you with many years of happiness and a string of little Legards to grace your years!"

"To Louis and Mattie!" echoed through the crowd of guests who had come to the hotel at Fayette for the reception and wedding feast.

Guy sat down, doing his best to keep jealousy at bay, but he couldn't help wishing he and Violet were the ones celebrating marriage. How he longed to see her, touch her, kiss her. But she was an ocean away, traveling through Great Britain with the Connellys. She would be in London by now, having already visited her employers' kin for a month in Ireland, and then the McAdams clan for a few days in Scotland while Mr. Connelly made a business call in Edinburgh.

Why did Violet have to be so far away? Reggie and Celina had come from Boston for the celebration, bringing Rose with them. It nearly broke Guy's heart to see them, and not see Violet, but perhaps it was for the best. He wanted desperately to make Violet his wife, but he was not yet ready. With his earnings from lumber camp and several weeks of work at the mill at Van's Harbor, he had been able to save enough to drill a well and buy a plow, a cultivator, and enough corn for planting his forty acres. With two draft horses borrowed from his father, he'd managed to plow his fields. Then, Joseph and Dan had helped him plant. He prayed that the summer would bring enough rain to make the corn grow. He would need to cultivate three or four times until the corn stalks were strong enough to be left alone. Meanwhile, he would work with his father making charcoal for Fayette. The furnaces were back in blast and ore was arriving regularly aboard the *W. P. Thew*. The town would be busy for a time. But Guy's hopes and dreams lay in his modest cabin outside the furnace village where he and Violet would one day make a life together.

The strains of a waltz played by Chase and his musician friends brought Guy's thoughts back to the present. He watched while Mr. Silverstone led his daughter onto the floor. Mattie was truly a beautiful bride, wearing a white satin gown garnished with lace across the bodice, and a train and veil that she held off the floor for dancing. When she and her father had circled the room, Louis cut in to claim his bride. Shortly after, guests joined them, filling the floor with a graceful flow of dancers. Joseph and Rose, Celina and Reggie, Lavinia and William, and Mr. McAdams with a gray-haired woman unfamiliar to Guy were among them. He couldn't help wondering who she was. Her stylish pale lilac costume could only have come from a big city department store.

Guy's curious thought came to an end when his sister Agnes urged him to take her around the floor. She talked as they danced.

"Did you notice the woman dancing with Mr. McAdams?"

"Oui. Who is she, do you know?"

Agnes's blue eyes sparkled. "Her name is Everilda McAdams. She's his brother's widow, and a wealthy one, at that. She came from Canada, near Windsor, for Mary's burial service in the middle of May. When she arrived, she said she was en route to British Columbia, then she decided to extend her stay in Fayette. Some folks are saying that when Mrs. McAdams leaves, Violet's grandfather will travel with her, and when they come back this way the Burleys will go with them to Canada."

Guy made no reply. Rumors often proved false over time, as had been the case when folks thought *he* would marry Mattie. But Guy couldn't help feeling some concern. If Violet's mother, step-father, and grandfather should move to Canada, would she want to settle there rather than on his little farm outside Fayette?

One year later
Saturday evening, June 20, 1891

The moment Violet saw the limestone bluff at the entrance to Snail-Shell Harbor, she knew she was home. Nothing she had seen in her travels to the East Coast and abroad could compare to the sense of belonging aroused within at the sight of Fayette. How thankful she was that a year ago, her kin had declined the strong urgings of her great-aunt to move to Canada and some strange place that she had never seen.

Standing on the deck of the *Corona* alongside Rose, Celina, and Reggie, she scoured the dusky shoreline for Guy, Grandpa, her mother, or anyone else she might recognize after an eighteen-month absence from Fayette. Her heartbeat quickened, her palms dampened, and she silently prayed that the affections exchanged by mail would be lived out in person now that she and Guy would be together once again.

Suddenly, Rose pointed. "They're coming down the hill! Mama, Papa Burley, Dan, and Grandpa! Right behind them are Flora and Sven and their little ones. And look over there! It's Guy, Joseph, Louis, and Mattie with her baby!"

Violet began to wave.

Her relatives waved back, and so did Guy, with wide sweeps of his arm.

In moments, she was off the boat and sharing hugs with her mother, brother, aunt, uncle, cousins, and grandfather. She marveled at how much the children had grown, and then her grandfather nudged her toward Guy, who stood a few feet away.

Tentatively, they moved toward one another. Guy had never looked so strong and handsome. Even in the fading light of dusk, she could see the ruggedness of his shoulders from the hard work of lumbering, milling, and farming. The ruddiness of his suntanned face contrasted sharply with the tenderness in his blue-eyed gaze.

Guy thought Violet had never looked so fetching. Her red hair formed a mass of lovely curls, setting off dark eyes that seemed to speak of excitement, longing, and even uncertainty. He reached for her hands, taking both of them in his and saying quietly, "You're finally here, *ma petite amie.*"

Violet's pulse raced. "Here to stay," she replied softly while her heart screamed love.

Suddenly, his arms enfolded her, holding her so tight, she was sure he could feel the stays of her corset pressing against his ribs as they crushed her own.

When he released her, her grandfather said, "Come up to the house, everyone! We'll have tea."

Celina, Reggie, and the Silverstones declined, preferring instead to start for home, but the others complied, except William who remained to haul trunks and bags aboard his wagon.

How wonderful it was to enter the front door and know that she had reached her destination at last. While her mother went to the kitchen to brew the tea, Violet settled with Guy on one end of the sofa, and Rose and Joseph sat on the other with Blackie leaping up to join them. Flora and Sven took the love seat while their children played on the floor nearby, and Grandpa and Dan brought dining chairs for Lavinia and William.

Violet hadn't been in the room long before noticing something about it seemed not quite the same. Then she realized that the lacy curtains on the front window had been replaced by heavy velvet. When she inquired about the change, her grandfather offered an enigmatic smile. Then Flora said rather irritably, "When Aunt Everilda was here last summer, she insisted on new window dressing."

Grandpa said, "She wanted to redecorate the entire parlor. I refused to allow it, so she turned her attention to the Maple Room where your great-grandmother used to live."

Dan said, "You should see it. It doesn't look one bit the same. Aunt Everilda renamed it the Rose Room."

Flora said, "But I call it Aunt Everilda's Folly."

"Is that so?" Violet replied. "Then I'll have to go and see it." She started for the back of the house. Guy and Blackie followed her through the kitchen where her mother was filling a platter with cookies, to the door that entered the back room. The first difference Violet noticed was on the face of the door. A sign—one that her father had made in the shape of a maple leaf with the word "Welcome" on it—was missing. Now, a plaque carved with a rose hung in

193

its place.

Violet turned to her mother "Where's Papa's sign?"

"Flora has it, dear," her mother replied.

As Violet proceeded into the room, Mr. Burley arrived at the back door with bags and trunks. While Guy helped him carry them inside, Violet studied the room that had originally been decorated with a theme of maple leaves for her great-grandmother. Now, from ceiling to floor, not a maple leaf could be found. Instead, cabbage roses dominated.

The walls had been papered with a cabbage rose print, covering the border of maple leaves that had been stenciled there years ago. The wardrobe that had sported maple leaves on the doors had been replaced with one of carved roses. The floor was different, too. Where maple leaves had decorated each corner, roses now bloomed. The small hand-hooked rug sporting one large maple leaf in the center had disappeared in favor of a big area rug with an overall pattern of cabbage roses. The plain pine bedstead was gone too, along with the quilt that had been hand-sewn by her great-grandmother in various shades of fall maple leaves. Now, a fancy black iron bed occupied one wall of the room, covered with a chenille spread tufted with roses. The maple leaf pillows had also vanished. Instead, rose-topped pillows stood plumped at the head of the bed.

Violet's gaze turned to the back wall. The old nine-pane window with a stained-glass maple leaf in the center pane had been completely replaced. A larger twelve-pane window now faced the backyard, but the landscape could not be seen through the stained-glass roses that decorated every piece of glass. Such a window needed no curtains, so gone were the curtains with maple leaves on their hems, and gone too were the tiebacks that had sported maple leaves on their faces.

The occasional chairs had not escaped Aunt Everilda's sweeping reforms, either. A small black chair that had been painted with golden maple leaves on its back was nowhere to be seen. Instead, a padded chair upholstered in a shade to match the deepest rose in the wallpaper stood in its place. Her great-grandmother's rocker had also been evicted, and a new one covered in rose chintz had materialized beside the parlor stove.

Troubled by the changes, Violet returned to her mother in the kitchen, accompanied by Guy, who carried a meowing Blackie under his arm. "Mama, what happened to all of the maple leaf things? The chairs, the rug, the wardrobe, the quilt, the pillows, and the window are all gone! And why didn't anyone mention it in their letters?"

Lavinia looked up from the tea tray she was arranging. "Flora and I have everything that Aunt Everilda replaced. You and Guy may have whatever you wish for your own home when you're ready, dear—except the window which Sven installed for Flora on her landing. As for telling you about the changes, you were in Europe. We seldom knew where to send a letter. Besides," her voice grew hushed, "the changes were quite a source of hard feelings for your grandpa and me at the time. There seemed no point in troubling you about it." Lavinia set spoons on the tray with the cups, saucers, and the teapot and handed it to Violet. "Help me serve, will you, please? I'll bring the cookies."

Violet did as asked. Pushing aside unkind thoughts of a great-aunt she had never met and changes she didn't like, she served the tea and resumed her place beside Guy on the sofa. Conversation centered on current concerns of the company town, not the least of which was a lack of demand for pig iron. The furnaces had not gone back into blast this spring as had been expected. With the stacks still cold, economic conditions were poor and the question of Fayette's future was very much on the minds of those who remained on the payroll, such as her grandfather, who was now tending to any job that needed doing at a reduced salary.

With Flora and Sven's children growing tired and cranky, discussion came to an end and the family departed. Guy, too, rose to take his leave. Violet saw him out, stepping onto the front porch to bid him good-bye in private. The night sky bathed them in starlight and moonbeams, and Violet could easily make out the face of the man she loved and the tenderness with which his gaze beheld her.

Guy enfolded her hands in his and smiled down at her. "It is so wonderful to have you back, *ma petite amie*, and near impossible to leave you." Bending to kiss her gently on the lips with a brush of his mustache, he asked, "Have you given thought to our wedding date?"

Violet nodded. "Late September. On the trip home, we all discussed it. Celina is going to stay in Michigan until we're wed, giving Rose the summer off. They're going to help me prepare. There is so much to get ready! A wedding dress, the house, our linens and—" She cut herself off, overwhelmed with the thought of it all.

Guy grinned. "Late September. It will be wonderful to have Celina and Rose here for a while." He kissed her fingertips. "I will come by tomorrow evening. *Je t'aime, ma petite amie.*"

"*Je t'aime,* Guy!"

Chapter

22

Two weeks before the wedding, September, 1891

"This morning, Violet, we'll go to the Company Store," stated Aunt Everilda in her customary, autocratic tone. "I want you to pick out whatever you need for your home—anything at all no matter the cost—and that will be my wedding gift to you. Afterward, we'll pay a call on your seamstress, Maggie, and see if the bodice of your wedding gown fits properly with her latest alterations." She raised a delicate china cup with her pinky finger extended, sipped the last of her breakfast tea, and then excused herself from the table. As the stately, gray-haired woman passed Violet on the way to the Rose Room, where she had been staying for the past ten days, she said, "Be ready in fifteen minutes, dear."

"Yes, ma'am," Violet replied sweetly, masking the resentment within. When she heard the door to the back room close, she turned to her sister with a look of dread.

Rose giggled quietly. "Looks like you're in for another morning of fun with Aunt Everilda." She kept her voice low.

"Oh, hush!" Violet scolded. "How I wish that woman would just go back where she came from."

Rose laughed out loud, her brown eyes dancing.

"There's not a chance of that until after your wedding."

"*My* wedding?" Violet fumed quietly. "Ever since she arrived, she's taken over. She overruled my choice of gold on cream for the engraved wedding invitations. Only silver on white would do. She's changed the style of my wedding veil three times. She's criticized the fit of the bodice twice. Three days ago, she ordered different lace trim for the train. I doubt it will even arrive in time for Maggie to make use of it."

Rose said, "And how do you like the parlor, now that she's redecorated it for your wedding?"

Violet sighed. "The changes to the parlor are somewhat irritating, but what bothers me even more is that she's forever haranguing Guy and me to move to Canada after we're married. 'It's so much better there, my dear,'" Violet said, imitating her aunt's snooty tone. "'Guy can make loads of money. You'll have a beautiful home and your children will be able to attend the finest of schools.'" Violet shook her head. "When will she realize that all we want is a modest life *here,* near Mama and Papa Burley, Dan, Grandpa, Louis and Mattie, Aunt Flora and Uncle Sven, and our other kin?"

Rose shrugged. "I don't think she's given up yet on Mama, Papa Burley, Dan, and Grandpa. She talks as if they'll be going to Canada with her when she leaves here."

Violet frowned. "I wish they'd set her straight on the matter."

"I don't suppose they want to rile her on the issue. You've seen how cantankerous she gets when anyone dares disagree with her."

"She's a regular a domestic dictator," Violet said disgustedly.

"But a wealthy and determined one," Rose observed.

"That's exactly the problem. She constantly uses her

money to get her own way, and no one seems to oppose her."

"Including you, even though you do a lot of complaining," Rose pointed out.

"It hardly seems worth the trouble to cross her. All this wedding business will pass. Once I'm married, she goes back to Canada, and Guy and I live our lives as we please without her interference."

Hearing the door to the Rose Room open, Violet's sister said, "You'd better get ready. I'll clear the table and wash up."

"Thanks, Sis." Violet gently squeezed Rose's shoulder before she left the table, thankful that at least her sister and her mother and Celina were constantly supportive during these patience-testing days with her great-aunt.

Hurrying up the stairs to the privacy of her bedroom, Violet dropped to her knees beside her bed, where Blackie had settled for a nap, and whispered a prayer. "God, help me to control my anger and my tongue. Let me appreciate Aunt Everilda's well-meaning intentions, even when I disagree with her suggestions. Thank you, Father. In the name of Jesus, Amen." Checking her appearance in the mirror, she took a deep breath and then headed down the stairs and out the door with her aunt.

At the Company Store, Violet was pleasantly surprised at Aunt Everilda's generosity and practicality. Even though the inventory of household goods was quite limited during these lean times for the Jackson Iron Company, an order could be placed for anything not available on the shelf, and her aunt made ample use of the service. A laundry boiler, cooking pots, mixing bowls, flour sifter, canisters, and lamps all made their way onto a list of items to come from Escanaba. Laundry soap, bar soap, a washboard, and staples such as flour, beans, sugar, and coffee would be delivered within the next few days. On their way out of the store, Violet thanked her aunt profusely.

Everilda smiled, her blue eyes full of affection. "It's my pleasure, dear. What benefit is there to being wealthy if one does not use that wealth to bless others? Now, let us go and see your seamstress."

An hour later, Violet returned home with her aunt, thankful that the bodice of her gown now fit perfectly, the veil had at last earned approval, and the lace for the train had arrived and was being sewn in place. The afternoon passed smoothly as well, attending to household chores with Rose, but when they joined their aunt and Blackie in the parlor to continue the work of embroidering towels and pillowcases, the older woman revived the topic that was most troublesome for Violet.

"I know you have told me that you have no interest in moving to Canada, but I do wish you would open your mind to the possibility." She paused to stroke Blackie, who lay purring on her lap. "Farming is so much more profitable there, than here on this limestone-infested peninsula. The rail line is easily accessible for transporting crops to market. In addition, when you and Guy start your family, your children will receive an excellent education with cultural benefits that can't be matched within a hundred miles of here." She gazed over the top of her magnifying eyeglasses in expectation of a response.

Blackie leaped down from her lap, and as if an ambassador for Everilda's cause, crossed the room to rub her face against Violet's skirt.

She picked up the cat and bit back angry words, loosing her tongue a moment later to make a soft reply. "If Guy should desire to take your suggestion and move to Canada,

I would not oppose him, but we have discussed your idea at length and are of one mind on the topic. We wish to remain here, in Michigan, near his family and mine."

"People move away from family and friends to take advantage of economic opportunities all the time," Aunt Everilda countered. "For example, your grandfather and grandmother moved here twenty-four years ago in hopes of a better life in the Jackson Iron Company's employ. Guy's family, too, came here at about that same time to supply charcoal for the J.I.C. But circumstances have changed. The company is failing. You knew it three years ago when you went East to work as a domestic. So did Celina and Rose. It's time to leave Fayette for good, my dear, whether you realize it or not."

Everilda's mention of Violet's decision to go East stirred a sense of deep resentment. At the same time, it was a difficult point to refute, challenging Violet's debating skills to the limit. After careful consideration, she crafted her response. "The company may be failing, but families still thrive hereabouts. Aunt Flora and Uncle Sven are reasonably successful on their farm, as are the Richbourgs and others who once worked for the J.I.C. Fishing is good, and lumbering, too, for those willing to go north of here where there are still good stands of timber. These folks don't seem to mind the lack of educational and cultural benefits to which you refer."

Aunt Everilda sighed. "I can see that I am just going to have to take this up with Guy again. Perhaps he has not become so set in his opinion that he is not willing to reconsider."

Resentment rose within. Violet's face grew warm and she was certain that a red stain bloomed on her cheeks. With great restraint, she molded her reply. "Let it drop, I beg you. Guy has made his decision. Another go-around won't win him over. It will only cause hard feelings."

Everilda's silver brow arched, but she said no more, leaving Violet uncertain as to the efficacy of her argument.

For the next several days, Violet put the topic from her mind to focus on linens for her new home, parlor decorations for the wedding ceremony, and the menu for the wedding breakfast to be held afterward at the hotel, another concession to her aunt, who was paying the cost.

With the wedding day near, Violet was at wit's end. Aunt Everilda thought nothing of changing her mind. She would agree to Violet's choices only to overrule them later, despite the difficulties that it caused others. Nothing seemed certain. Nothing, that is, except change.

Aside from wedding stress and strain, the Jackson Iron Company had initiated a systematic dismantling of its furnaces at Fayette. For several days now, her grandfather and other company employees had been engaged in the process, loading parts onto barges for shipment to Escanaba by boat, and then Negaunee by rail where they would be reconstructed. The certainty of the company's withdrawal from the Garden Peninsula had re-ignited strong efforts on the part of Aunt Everilda to convince her grandfather, mother, stepfather, and brother, to move to Canada and make a new start, although she had said nothing further to Guy. The most troubling aspect of the suggestion was that her relatives had led Aunt Everilda to believe they might take her up on the idea, while knowing full well they had no intention of going to Canada.

When Violet had questioned her mother about the deceptiveness, she had countered with an interesting reply.

"I've learned that where Aunt Everilda is concerned, it's best to fight one battle at a time. You've seen how much stress she has created while planning your wedding. Hopefully, we can wait until after you're married to set her straight on the question of moving to Canada."

Violet accepted her mother's explanation, though not thoroughly convinced of its wisdom.

Chapter

23

The day before the wedding

Violet rose late, finally giving in to Blackie's persistent efforts to rouse her with playful leaps across her blanket. Violet had been up into the wee hours, first talking with Guy at length about their future in the cabin on the farm, and then, embroidering until well past two in the morning because she was too excited to sleep. When she finally came down to breakfast, she expected to hear her aunt scolding her. Instead, Rose's sweet voice called her into the kitchen where she asked what she should make Violet for breakfast.

"A couple of poached eggs, and one of those delicious apple cinnamon muffins you baked yesterday would be wonderful," Violet replied. Seeing that the door to the Rose Room stood ajar, she checked there for her aunt to no avail. "Where is Aunt Everilda?"

Rose turned away, her answer uncharacteristically subdued. "She said to tell you she was going to the hotel to go over the arrangements for tomorrow."

"Did she say when she would be back, or that I should meet her there?"

Rose shook her head, placed a muffin on a plate, and

then proceeded to fill a pan with water for the eggs.

"Is something bothering you, Rose? You seem quieter than usual."

The sometimes-moody sixteen-year-old turned to her and put on a smile that held no sincerity. "I'm fine. Your eggs will be ready in a few minutes. Why don't you have a seat at the dining table."

Violet poured herself a cup of milk, carried it, and the muffin to the table, and sat down to enjoy a breakfast free from the strain of Aunt Everilda's domination. She was looking forward with happy anticipation to beginning her life as Guy's wife when Rose brought her two perfectly poached eggs.

"You're such a dear, getting breakfast for me like this," Violet said appreciatively.

"Celina has taught me well," Rose replied, pulling out a chair to sit across from her sister.

A little butter made the eggs slide down easily. Violet commented on the fine job Maggie had done creating her wedding gown, and the attractive lavender dress that Rose would wear while attending as maid of honor.

Rose said little and seemed distracted, winding a long strand of her red hair around her finger and then unwinding it time and again.

Violet assumed that the strain of living with Aunt Everilda while planning the wedding was taking its toll. Swallowing the last bite of muffin, she said, "I suppose I should go over to the hotel and learn what last minute changes Aunt Everilda has required for the wedding break-fast."

Rose quickly unwound the hair from her finger, saying, "I wouldn't do that, if I were you."

Violet stood and picked up her dishes. "But why not?

205

Aunt Everilda is probably vexed with me for sleeping late as it is."

"No, she's not!" Rose jumped up and hurried to take the dirty dishes from Violet. "I'll take care of these. You go into the parlor and do some embroidery. You are *not* to go to the hotel!"

"But why?"

"Because Aunt Everilda said so!" Rose's eyes suddenly filled with tears.

"What's the matter, Rose? What has you so upset? There must be something you're not telling me!"

Rose ignored her sister and headed for the kitchen, Violet and Blackie at her heels.

The younger girl set the dishes in the dry sink, picked up the cat, and turned to Violet, sobs halting her speech. "I fibbed … Aunt Everilda isn't at the hotel … she told me to tell you she was there so you wouldn't find out …" She buried her face in Blackie's fur.

Violet wrapped her arm about Rose and offered her a hanky. "There, now. Calm down and tell me what it is I'm not supposed to find out."

The younger girl set down the cat and dabbed her eyes. "Aunt Everilda went out to your cabin. She said she had some secret business to attend to there. She made me promise to say that she was at the hotel instead, so as not to raise your suspicions. Oh, Violet, I think she went there to insist that Guy should move with you to Canada!"

Violet's heart raced. "What makes you think that?"

"Mama and Papa came by to get her and drove her out there early this morning in Papa's wagon. I overheard them talking with Aunt Everilda last night in the Rose Room while you and Guy were in the parlor. I kept hearing the words 'move to Canada' and Guy's name. I think Mama and Papa have decided to move there and the three of them thought that together they could convince Guy that the two of you should move there, too!"

Anger surged within, sending a searing heat into Violet's cheeks. "I can't believe it! Betrayed by my own mother! I'm going out there right now and settle the matter!"

"I'll come with you!"

Violet shook her head. "You stay here. Celina said she'd drop by today. If she comes while I'm gone, please tell her I'm sorry I missed her, and the reason."

Rose nodded.

Within a few minutes, Violet had rented a horse from the livery and started for the cabin. She had not visited there for several days, kept away by Guy and her mother who had insisted on preparing the place for her while she attended to wedding details in town with her aunt. Anger and heartbreak battled within. By the time she was in sight of the cabin, anger was winning, and a supply of words waited on her tongue for their target. Aunt Everilda came out of the cabin just as Violet dismounted.

The older woman smiled broadly. "Violet, my dear! I wasn't expecting to see you here!"

"How *dare* you?" Violet angrily demanded.

"Beg your pardon?" Lines etched the older woman's forehead.

Guy appeared in the doorway behind Everilda, confusion evident in his expression.

Violet stepped face to face with her aunt and continued. "How *dare* you enlist the help of my mother and stepfather to change Guy's mind about living in Canada?"

Guy shook his head and pressed his finger to his lips.

Violet ignored him and sped on. "Since the day of your

arrival you have done nothing but make trouble, insisting on your own way in every detail of my wedding plans, making changes to Grandpa's house that were neither needed nor wanted. You've convinced Mama and Papa to move to Canada, and now the three of you are determined to convince Guy to do the same!"

"Nonsense!" retorted the older woman. "Your mother and William are not moving to Canada, and I have said not one word to Guy of moving there, either. Come inside and you shall see that our purposes here are quite to the contrary."

When Violet hesitated, Everilda and Guy flanked her on either side, ushering her by the elbows through the cabin door that now displayed her great-grandmother's maple leaf plaque that said, "Welcome."

With a sweep of her arm, Everilda said, "*This* is where you shall live, my dear. Take a good look, and tell me if it is to your liking."

At first glance, Violet could see that the cabin had been expanded at the rear. In addition, the entire place had been furnished with far more than the maple leaf castoffs from her grandparents' home and the items she had chosen at the store.

In the kitchen stood her mother. She looked up from the table where she was placing silverware in a drawer, her brown eyes aglow with excitement. "Come and see what your aunt has given you!" She indicated a fully stocked china cabinet in the corner.

Upon close inspection, Violet discovered a gorgeous display of violet-patterned dinnerware, the likes of which she had never seen. On the walls hung two new cupboards with glass doors that revealed a set of everyday enamelware including plates, cups, bowls, and pitchers. Beneath one of the cupboards, a small icebox had been installed, and beneath the other was a potato bin. Cooking pots hung from hooks in an overhead beam. Her flour sifter and mixing bowls waited on the shelf beneath the table, along with her canisters.

Violet's head moved slowly from side to side. She turned to Aunt Everilda. "I'm so sorry! I had no idea! Can you ever forgive me?"

The older woman smiled. "Of course, my dear." Placing an arm about Violet's shoulders, she pointed toward the back of the cabin. "Let us look at your new sleeping area."

Violet shifted her gaze to discover William kneeling beside a double bed, tightening the ropes. She hurried to take a closer look. On the bed's thick mattress lay a wedding quilt composed of squares made by the ladies of Fayette. Her great-grandmother's maple leaf quilt, too small for a bed this size, had been turned into a dressing screen.

Making one last turn of the rope adjuster, William rose to his feet, smiling proudly. "I made ye this bed. Your great-grandma's pine bed was too small for a married couple. Think the two of ya can sleep tight on this?"

Violet pressed her hand into the soft mattress, feeling the firmness of the rope support beneath. "We'll sleep just fine here. Thank you, Papa Burley! I was afraid we would be sleeping on the floor until we could afford a bed!"

Guy came alongside her. "Did you notice the other things that had been your great-grandmother's?" He pointed to the window behind the bed.

There hung the curtains that had a maple leaf border, held open with the special maple leaf tiebacks. On the floor in front of the bed lay the small hooked rug with the maple leaf in the center, and beside the bed stood the wardrobe with the maple leaf door.

Everilda led her next to the sitting area. There, her grandmother's rocker and the smaller black chair painted with the golden maple leaves shared space with an over-stuffed chair large and comfortable enough for a man. Everilda ran her hand over the rugged brown corduroy upholstery. "Guy picked out this chair—a gift from me. I argued vociferously for leather upholstery but he insisted on cotton. So you see, I don't always insist on my own way!"

Regret for earlier words still plagued Violet. "I can see now that I was so wrong."

The older woman smiled. "You spoke from the heart, and you spoke the truth about wanting my way in the details of your wedding, and the redecorating of Angus's parlor. But where did you ever get the wrongheaded notion that your mother, stepfather, and I came out here to try to convince Guy to move to Canada?"

"Rose said she overheard the three of you talking last night," Violet replied.

Everilda exchanged glances with Lavinia and William, and they all laughed. Then Violet's aunt explained. "Rose *did* hear us talking about moving to Canada. What she *did-n't* hear was what was said beforehand. Your mother had speculated on how ironic it would be if, after all our efforts to expand this cabin and furnish it as your newlywed nest, Guy decided that the two of you were going to leave Fayette and move to Canada. Of course, I followed that with the comment that William and she would have to move, too, if that were the case."

Guy stepped close. Taking Violet's hands in his, he gazed tenderly into the sparkling brown eyes of the one he loved and longed for. "I hope you know by now that I would never make such a decision without your approval, *ma petite amie."*

Violet sighed. "I should have known."

Everilda said, "I believe that puts a good end on this story. Now, let's all go and have lunch at the hotel, my treat. By the time we get to town, Angus will be leaving work for the midday meal, and he and Rose can join us. Besides, I want to check with the hotel staff to make sure all is in order for the wedding breakfast tomorrow."

With agreement unanimous, Violet reluctantly left the cabin that would soon be her home. Guy's comforting arm tight about her waist, she headed for the livery horse for the last leg of her journey toward wedded bliss.

Chapter

24

The atmosphere was joyful as everyone gathered about a large table at the hotel and placed their orders. But something about Grandpa McAdams' smile seemed unconvincing. Violet wondered if he was mourning the fact that his beloved wife of so many years had not lived to enjoy the happy occasion of the upcoming nuptials. Violet was expecting words to that effect when she asked him what was on his mind.

"I have an announcement to make," he replied. After a slight pause, his countenance grew as solemn as Violet had ever seen it, and when he continued, his downhearted tone conveyed his deep concern. "Today is my last day in the Jackson Iron Company's employ. This afternoon, we'll load the last of the furnace parts on a barge. Tomorrow, Superintendent Saunders leaves with them for Escanaba, and then Negaunee. There will be nothing left but some scrap iron that the Chicago Bolt and Nut Company will salvage." He hung his head and Violet thought he was about to cry.

Lavinia was the first to speak. "I'm so sorry, Papa, but we all knew it was coming."

Everilda said, "And sooner rather than later, I might add."

Rose said, "Have you decided what you'll do next?"

Guy said, "You're welcome to live with Violet and me."

Angus shook his head. "I could never do that. It's hard enough starting out, just the two of you."

Lavinia said, "You know you always have a place with William and me if you want, Papa."

He acknowledged the offer with an appreciative nod.

Everilda said, "Come to Canada! I've been trying to convince you to move back across the border for over a year. Now is the perfect time. But first, we'll go out west, like I did last year. I want to show you how beautiful the mountains are in the fall. Then, when we return, you can be the lord of my manor. After all, you are a Canadian, born and raised."

Violet shuddered at the thought that her grandfather might move away and take this overbearing woman as his wife.

Angus smiled. "Everilda, your invitation is generous and quite romantic, but one thing I know. At my age, I lack the grit necessary to be the lord of your manor. I have a different plan, one that seems best suited for all concerned." Again, he paused.

Rose grew impatient. "Tell us what it is, Grandpa!"

His smile widened. "I'll be moving out to Flora and Sven's within a couple of days. They can use my help on their farm. Once the crops are in, we'll put an addition on their house so I won't be under foot."

Violet said, "I'm so glad you'll be nearby, Grandpa."

Angus raised a finger. "Most of the time. I've been thinking. With the furnaces shut down for good, I could make some extended trips across the bay to see Toby and Elin and their children from time to time. I'll go when I'm not needed by Sven and Flora."

William said, "God love it, ye had a plan all the time, and a right good one at that. Now we have two reasons to celebrate tomorrow. Guy and Violet start a new life, and so do ye, Angus McAdams!" He raised his water glass. "To new beginnings!"

"To new beginnings," echoed around the table, glasses clinking, but Angus's smile soon faded, and Violet could sense the toll taken by the termination of his employment.

Violet's wedding day, Thursday, September 24, 1891

Her grandfather's problems were far from Violet's mind the following morning when sun streaked into her window and Blackie leaped onto her bed to awaken her. She arose to get a bite to eat and prepare for her wedding. Aunt Everilda had insisted that she bathe and dress in the Rose Room where every detail could be carefully overseen. Her mother and sister had wisely chosen to keep their distance while Violet donned her wedding costume with the assistance of her bossy aunt. Though tense with anticipation, Everilda showed a sweet and gentle side hitherto unseen. She nevertheless maintained supreme dominance and a scrupulous attention to detail.

Time passed so quickly that before Violet knew it, she was standing in front of the large mirror her aunt had installed on the inside of the wardrobe door, taking in the full effect of the gown and veil that had undergone countless alterations. It was almost as if Violet were looking at some other young woman—one of sophistication and elegance. Her long-sleeved, white peau de soie gown included a full, lace-trimmed train. The bodice was draped diagonally with lace in the latest Paris fashion. Her tulle veil included a narrow edge of the same lace, and was fastened on with white violet blossoms. The one concession of color to the entirely white costume was the small corsage at her left shoulder that included tiny silk violet blossoms, a gift from Guy that had been approved and even adopted by Aunt Everilda as the theme for all of the wedding decorations.

Standing beside her in a rose pink gown of the latest fashion, Everilda smiled at Violet's image in the mirror. "You are likely the most beautiful bride this town will ever see, my dear."

Violet blushed. "Only because of your good counsel and generosity, Aunt Everilda."

"I was only too glad to do it, my dear."

Violet was reflecting on her aunt's masterful arrangements for this special day when the clock on her dresser chimed the hour, and the woman spoke with quiet excitement.

"It is time to go out now. God bless you, my dear." With a tear in her eye, she opened the door to find that Angus was waiting patiently on the other side, and then she headed for the parlor.

Violet's grandfather gazed at her with a look so full of love and approval that she thought he was going to cry. Then, the strains from Chase's violin floated down the hallway. Placing her hand on his arm, he led her to the open door of the parlor. There, they paused, and Violet could see that all eyes were focused on them. At her aunt's prompting, she remembered to smile for the witnesses gathered— Guy's parents, his brother Louis and sister-in-law Mattie, his sister Celina and brother-in-law Reggie, his brother Joseph, and her own mother, sister, brother, and stepfather.

Then her gaze locked with Guy's. She had never seen him so handsome. He wore a white tie and white shirt with a charcoal gray vested suit. His hair and mustache had been barber trimmed and his cheeks and chin were freshly shaved. The tenderness in his blue eyes held enough love to last a lifetime.

The moment Violet had come into view Guy's heart had thumped so loudly, he was certain others had noticed it pounding beneath his jacket. Her loveliness took his breath away and set his normally steady hands to trembling. All his years of waiting for Violet had finally brought them to this triumphal moment when their dreams of a lifetime together would be realized. Taking a deep breath, he calmed his heart and mind, ready for the promises that would seal their love.

With Celina as matron of honor and Louis as best man, vows were exchanged in the presence of family, and the entire company adjourned to the wedding breakfast that awaited them at the hotel. Carriages hired by Aunt Everilda carried the wedding party and immediate family the short distance to the center of town where friends and neighbors were gathering for the wedding reception and breakfast.

The hotel dining room had never looked finer. Every table included lovely arrangements of violet blossoms. Name cards engraved in silver on white marked each place. Along one wall, a cake stacked high with many tiers was topped with a spray of butter cream violets. On the table beside it, a mound of wedding gifts awaited the newlyweds.

Violet was too excited to have an appetite for the creamed whitefish on toast, but she did enjoy the fresh citrus fruit served in cups, and the *soleil et lune* breakfast cake. Her wedding cake, too, held special appeal. Its French vanilla flavor and frothy butter cream frosting suited her perfectly. When she had spoken with each of her guests, some thirty in all, Guy drove her and Celina and Reggie back to her grandfather's house. There, with Celina's help, she removed her wedding gown and put on a forest green dress decorated with large cream colored bows on each shoulder. The going away dress was hardly necessary. She and Guy had foregone the idea of a honeymoon preferring instead to go immediately to their cabin to begin their life together as a farming couple with a corn crop to harvest. But Aunt Everilda had insisted on giving her the dress, and so Violet had acquiesced.

Tucking the last of her belongings into her trunk, Violet watched while the fellows carried it out to Guy's wagon. Then, turning to Celina, who along with Rose and Reggie would be departing for Boston come morning, she offered a hug and fond words of farewell. Guy, too, bid his sister good-bye and saw her to the carriage. Together they waved as Reggie set the rig in motion and disappeared down the street.

Then Guy reached for Violet's hand and turned her toward him. Pulling her into his arms, he covered her mouth with his for their first lingering kiss as husband and wife while Blackie circled them, meowing approval. When their lips parted, he spoke tenderly. *"Ma petite amie,* are you ready to depart for your new home?"

"Almost," Violet replied. "Will you please drive me down to the dock? I want to take one last look at this town."

"Of course," Guy replied, helping her up into the seat of his wagon. "But it won't be your *last* look. We'll be back tomorrow to haul our wedding gifts home, and we'll come to town once a week or more thereafter to visit the store and post office."

"I know," Violet replied, "but it will never be the same after today."

Her words made Guy realize the dual significance of this day. While he and his new wife were celebrating a joyous new beginning, others including her grandfather were mourning the death of a once thriving pig iron industry.

Melancholy gripped Violet as the wagon came to a halt alongside the dock below her grandfather's house. Gazing at the saltbox perched on the hill, she could hardly believe that her beloved grandfather would soon have to move forever from the place that held so many wonderful memories of her childhood and growing-up years. Tea parties with her grandmother, family gatherings at holidays, consoling love and shelter after her father's death, and the turbulent coming-of-age years were inextricably connected with that small but loving home. And today, she had added one more memory to the collection—the most important memory of all—her wedding. A tear sprang to her eye, and she quickly dried it with the back of her hand, turning away to take in the view of the furnace, Company Store, and Town Hall. She could hear yet the clang of steel on iron as "moulders" hired to work in the casting houses broke iron pigs from the sow. She could see the "cinders," the hefty men hired to do the hauling, carting the pigs to the dock. And she could smell the furnace smoke that rose above the town, overspreading it with black soot and the foul fragrance of industry.

For a moment, she remembered how much she had hated this town after her father's death. The passing of years now revealed to her a new truth. It wasn't the town that she had hated after all, but the painful loss of her father that had made her think that way.

And then, she heard the silence of cold furnaces and saw the steamer departing with Uncle Toby's family and others forced to find fresher fields elsewhere. The pain of that parting came again to mind as if it were yesterday.

Gazing at his new wife, Guy wondered about the

218

thoughts that brought such a sorrowful look to her lovely countenance and tears to her sad brown eyes. Slipping his arm about her waist, he pulled her close and offered a handkerchief.

Guy's embrace made Violet realize that the time had come to send sad memories fleeing. This was the happiest day of her life. This was *her* time to leave Fayette and start anew. Guy slapped the reins and started for home, *their* home, where a life of farming and a future filled with his fond affection waited.

But as they rolled up the hill leading from town, she couldn't resist one last look over her shoulder.

Guy was right. Though they were leaving Fayette today, they would be back tomorrow, and on many days to come. The furnaces may be dead, but Fayette would live on.

ABOUT DONNA WINTERS

Donna adopted Michigan as her home state in 1971 when she moved from a small town in upstate, New York. She began penning romance novels in 1982 and celebrated the release of her first published book in 1985. To date, three publishers have released a total of sixteen titles by Donna.

She currently lives in Michigan's Upper Peninsula with her husband and canine family members. There, she continues to research and write stories inspired by the natural beauty and fascinating history of the region.

Donna loves to hear from her readers. You may contact her by visiting *greatlakesromances.com* and clicking on the *E Mail Us* button, or by writing to her at the address below.

Donna Winters
4555 II Road
Garden, Michigan 49835

Author Donna Winters and friends outside the
Machine Shop at Fayette Historic State Park.

More *Great Lakes Romances*®
Order online at *greatlakesromances.com*
Or contact
Bigwater Publishing
4555 II Road
Garden, MI 49835

MACKINAC TRILOGY by Donna Winters
Mackinac, First in the series of *Great Lakes Romances*® (Set at Grand Hotel, Mackinac Island, 1895.)
The Captain and the Widow, Second in the series of *Great Lakes Romances*® (Set in South Haven, Michigan, 1897.)
Sweethearts of Sleeping Bear Bay, Third in the series of *Great Lakes Romances*® (Set in the Sleeping Bear Dune region of northern Michigan, 1898.)

LIGHTHOUSE TRILOGY by Donna Winters
Charlotte of South Manitou Island, Fourth in the series of *Great Lakes Romances* ® (Set on South Manitou Island, Michigan, 1891-1898)
Aurora of North Manitou Island, Fifth in the series of *Great Lakes Romances*® (Set on North Manitou Island, Michigan, 1898-1899.)
Bridget of Cat's Head Point, Sixth in the series of *Great Lakes Romances*® (Set in Traverse City and the Leelanau Peninsula of Michigan, 1899-1900.)
A SPIN-OFF by Donna Winters
Rosalie of Grand Traverse Bay, Seventh in the series of *Great Lakes Romances*® (Set in Traverse City, Michigan, and Winston-Salem, North Carolina, 1900.)

Fayette Trilogy by Donna Winters
(Three stories set in the former iron smelting town of Fayette in

Michigan's Upper Peninsula)
Fayette—A Time to Love, Eighth in the series of *Great Lakes Romances*® (Set in 1869)
Fayette—A Time to Laugh, Ninth in the series of *Great Lakes Romances*® (Set in 1879)
Fayette—A Time to Leave, Tenth in the series of *Great Lakes Romances*® (Set in 1885-1891)

Isabelle's Inning, Encore Edition #1 in the series of *Great Lakes Romances*® (Set in the heart of Great Lakes Country, 1903.)

MICHIGAN WILDERNESS ROMANCES
by Donna Winters
Jenny of L'Anse Bay, Special Edition in the series of *Great Lakes Romances*® (Set in the Keweenaw Peninsula of Upper Michigan in 1867.)
Elizabeth of Saginaw Bay, Pioneer Edition in the series of *Great Lakes Romances*® (Set in the Saginaw Valley of Michigan, 1837.)

TWO CHICAGO STORIES—*reprints of old classics*
***Sweet Clover—A Romance of the White City* by Clara Louise Burnham**, Centennial Edition in the series of *Great Lakes Romances*® (Set in Chicago at the World's Columbian Exposition of 1893.)
***Amelia* by Brand Whitlock**, Encore Edition #2 in the series of *Great Lakes Romances*® (Set in Chicago and Springfield, Illinois, 1903.)

CALEDONIA CHRONICLES by Donna Winters
Unlikely Duet—Caledonia Chronicles—Part 1 in the series of *Great Lakes Romances*® (Set in Caledonia, Michigan, 1905.)
Butterfly Come Home—Caledonia Chronicles—Part 2 in the series of *Great Lakes Romances*® (Set in Caledonia and Calumet, Michigan, 1905-06.)

***Bigwater Classics™* Series**
Great Lakes Christmas Classics, A Collection of Short Stories, Poems, Illustrations, and Humor from Olden Days
Snail-Shell Harbor, a reprinted novel from 1870 about Fayette, Michigan, and the iron smelting days.